Girls Count

by Mary Hlastala

This book is a fictional memoir inspired by real events. It reflects the author's recollections of experiences over time. For dramatic and narrative purposes, this book contains fictionalized scenes, locations, and dialogue, composite and representative characters, and time compression.

Part One

1

"Will this be on the test?"

I look down at my worn-out yellow Converse to hide my uncontrollable eye roll. Why does every class end up with some guy in the front row asking if what we learned will be on the test? "Everything we have discussed in class is a concept the professor wants us to know and should be fair game. Please accept that," I think to myself. I hate that question.

This is my last year in the math program, but I'm still surprised at the way guys will yell out questions like that. I suppose they're trying to seem prepared for what lies ahead, but I see it as laziness. Questions like this come from a student who doesn't want to learn anything they don't need to. It seems to be a guy that will ask it every time, too. Maybe some girls are afraid to ask.

Professor Mason's class is hard enough without the lecture being interrupted with questions like this. Every now and again someone will inquire about something that is so off topic and clearly a discussion for office hours. Each class is an overwhelming amount of information. We don't have time for students to interject with their thoughts on the material. I guess there's hope among some students that we can actually think deeply about the concepts, but unfortunately the college math experience isn't designed that way. We come in, look straight ahead, absorb as much as we can, and try to make it through to the final exam. Then it's onto the next class that will feel just as stressful.

It's also hard because I've been one of the few girls in each class I've taken at Strauss University. There's a shift when it's a social science class or one of the core classes that all students are required to take, but otherwise I mostly hear the male perspective when it comes to mathematics. Feeling isolated in a math class doesn't make it easy. I'm always hopeful on the first day of classes that there will be more female voices. Walking into a new classroom I think that this will be the class where the gender gap has shifted. Day one arrives: three girls and twenty-seven guys. Nope. Maybe next time.

My saving grace has been Miranda. Ever since our freshman year, Miranda and I have stuck together, trying our best to keep the same class schedules. It took us a week to start talking to each other on that first day of classes. We were both trying to play it cool, like we weren't terrified to be in college, especially in the math program. I had been out of school for four years. I took a break after high school because I didn't know what life plan I was to make at the ripe old age of eighteen. Most people saw it as laziness or apathy. I thought, instead, that I was being responsible by not wasting time or money on a degree I may never use. Miranda, on the other hand, was a free-spirited artsy type who spent a year at art school before she transferred here to get a degree in math. This was a total surprise to most of her friends and family.

After the panic of that first week, I sought out one of the only other girls in the class. A creature of habit, Miranda always sat in the same corner desk in the back of the classroom. I came in early one day and grabbed the desk next to hers. As soon as she came in she dropped down her quilted blue and green bag and started taking out her collection of colorful pens. I couldn't help but watch her all through class, flipping back and forth through her notes, adding pink in the margins, underlining in blue, the professor's words in red. I was hooked.

Since we're planning to graduate at the end of the spring term, we promised to help each other with assignments and vowed to always make time to study together. Miranda was particularly worried about Professor Mason's class. His take-no-prisoners teaching style didn't instill the most confidence in his students. He was cold, he wrote as fast as he talked, and sometimes he treated us like grad students preparing for the Master's Exam rather than undergrads just trying to survive.

"Alice, are we still meeting after class on Friday to study?" Miranda has a slight panic in her voice after class.

"Yep. Let's meet in the Brandford Hall study lounge," I suggest. My reassuring smile is one that

Miranda has seen many times before. As we walk out of class together, front-row-boy brushes past us and stops at the coffee cart outside the main door.

"Does he always have to ask if something is gonna be on the test?" Miranda asks, rolling her eyes. I can't help but laugh.

By the time I get home, Cullen has his head down, pen poised, and a look of determination and focus that I often see when he's at his desk. He's usually writing music or strumming on his guitar when I come home after six o'clock, having the luxury of the house all to himself. Our one-bedroom starter home seemed so quaint when we bought it last year. Now it seems much smaller with our years of odds and ends filling every available square inch. It took us so long to find a house because the Portland housing market didn't allow a young couple like us to find a place that fit our needs. We struggled for months and finally settled on the one place that we could actually live in. One house we looked at didn't have a kitchen floor and one had floors that were so warped it was like walking in a funhouse. Even though it's small, we've made the best of this little home, although the tight quarters make it hard for us to have our own personal space.

Cullen and I have been together for six years and I'm so glad I have someone to come home to who I can talk to about school, or really anything that's on my mind. He's been so supportive along the way. When we met I had no plans to go to college, but I was so unhappy working at a corporate retail job that when they went out of business it made sense for me to make a big life change.

"Hey baby, how was class?" Cullen asks without looking up from his notebook. "What did front-row-boy ask today?" He knows all too well that I have an update on my day at school.

"He asked, 'Will this be on the test?'" I inform him.

"Better than asking for a situation where the theorem doesn't work," he replies.

"Yeah, that question drives me so crazy. I don't understand why he needs to know when a theorem *doesn't* work," I say with a touch of frustration in my voice. "We learn the theorems in order to use them, not question them."

"I'm sorry. That seems annoying," he says, trying to understand my mini rant. "Well, dinner is on the stove. I'm gonna work for a little while longer."

"Sounds good. I have some homework to do tonight," I added, determined to commit to working by saying it out loud. It's hard to study after class because I'm usually too tired to work when I get home. I'm mentally exhausted from sitting in class and having to get back into math mode and focus on homework can be a challenge. As I leave Cullen to his work, I set down my bag, hang up my raincoat in the mudroom, then lift the lid of the pot on the stove to check its contents. Grabbing a bowl from the cabinet I scoop out a heaping pile of chili and hit the couch for a few minutes in front of the TV to turn my brain off. Rick Moranis, our plus-sized tuxedo cat, takes no time to jump up on my lap and settle in for what he hopes will be a long winter's nap. (Always calling my bluff, Cullen accepted the name Rick Moranis after I told him when we met that I thought this would be a hilarious name for a pet.)

"I should create an ultimate Flonkerton championship," I mutter to myself while watching a rerun of The Office. It was the Office Olympics and Jim and Pam were creating office games. Flonkerton, also known as the Icelandic sport of box-of-paper-snowshoe-racing, seems like a great way to pass the time. I bet it's also a great workout. Miranda and I could be teammates and represent the Pacific Northwest division. It's so easy to get lost in a TV show, especially when Rick Moranis is on my lap. He's so warm and cuddly that I hate to disturb him. Okay, I have to get some work done. Pulling Rick Moranis off my lap he melts into a pile of fur, seemingly void of bones, and I gently place him on the couch in the warm spot I'm leaving behind. I grab my backpack from where I left it by the front door and pull out my notebook of disjointed theorems and symbols. Suddenly the sounds from Cullen's guitar start to fill the room as he begins to work out a new chord change. I fear that this repetitive noise coming from the bedroom will keep me from focusing. I hate to interrupt him when he's working, but I really need to study.

"Hey, are you gonna be in here for a while?" I ask, slowly creeping open the door.

"Yeah, probably. I want to work this out before

band practice this weekend. Is it bothering you?"

"A little, yeah." I try to sound apologetic. "I have to study." Cullen is always getting kicked out of the house and it makes me feel guilty since we have such a small place. Now it occurs to me why couples don't settle for one-bedrooms. We never planned to have kids, so it made sense at the time. Now I'm not so sure.

"Well, how about I go to the garage?" Cullen suggests.

"That would be great. Thanks, hon."

There's a buzzing sound coming from the depths of my bag. Looking at my phone I see that Miranda is texting to ask how I worked out number twelve on the homework assignment. I tell her that I'm just about to get started but I'll let her know when I get there. It seems like she went home and got straight to work. Maybe Jacob was working late. Her fiancé, head chef at a vegan restaurant downtown, often didn't get home until after ten o'clock leaving Miranda a peaceful place to work. She has an easier time diving into her work and can spend hours studying without a break. I, however, usually have a couch calling my name and a cat in desperate need of attention.

Getting to my desk, I clear off a small pile of magazines that are water-warped from the coffee I spilled last week. It's probably time I dispose of these since I rarely have time to look at them anyway. It takes me a few minutes to get motivated, but I commit to working for one full hour. That's usually as much as I can do before my brain starts to hurt. By the time I get to number twelve, I text Miranda and hope that my proof lines up with hers. We've been in Mason's class for almost seven weeks, but it's still hard to figure out exactly what he's looking for. He grades pretty hard and his feedback is often vague. After almost ten minutes of trying to make sense of the problem, we finally agree on a solution then I'm back to working on my own.

As much as it bothers me in class, it makes sense that students are trying to engage in a conversation about math. We sit here for hours by ourselves trying to make sense of all this but we never get to discuss it. Mason talks at us for most of the class period while standing at the front of the room and writing endless notes on the board. It's no wonder that most of us have such a hard time understanding what he's talking about. There isn't any context. I don't know how or when I will ever be able to apply these theorems in a real way. It's disappointing that a subject I love so much is taught in such a cold and incomprehensible way.

I strain my neck to look at the clock on the stove in the kitchen. The neon green numbers tell me that I'm fifty-eight minutes into studying. Probably a good time to take a break.

The rain is strumming on the window as I fill the teapot with water in the kitchen and I can no longer see the backyard through the darkness. There are just silhouettes and shadows cast from the light outside the garage door. As I grab a tea bag from the box, smelling the mixture of orange and ginger, Rick Moranis rubs against my legs, looking for attention. Happy to give him some love, I rub his head and he lays down on the cold floor, stretched out in an arc so I can reach his belly. He's a sucker for belly rubs and I happily give in to his request. On cold nights like this, it's hard not to do anything but curl up on the couch with him. Rick Moranis will follow me around the room, waiting for me to settle in so he can do the same. After the teapot makes its alarming screech, I get lost in the aroma of the tea as I pour the water into my cup and begin to feel the warmth of the steam hitting my face. Before I know it, I'm under the velvety throw blanket and Rick Moranis isn't far behind. I know I should be studying right now, but the comfort of the couch and my little friend on my lap makes it easy to ignore that.

It's almost nine o'clock when I hear Cullen come in through the back door. I assure him that I put in a good hour doing homework (minus two minutes) and his need to leave the house was not in vain. I pull back the blanket so he can join me, causing Rick Moranis to reposition at our feet and locking us into position so we don't disturb him once he falls asleep.

In the morning I wake up feeling rested but a little anxious about the amount of work I need to get done. Maybe I should have tried a little harder to study last night. Luckily I don't have any classes so I'll be able to study for most of the day today. Cullen left for work early, probably around seven o'clock. I barely remember his kiss on the cheek when he left this morning as I was in and out of sleep. Rick Moranis usually gets moving around 5:30 A.M right before Cullen's alarm clock goes off, but I'm always happy to see him back at my feet when I wake, a warm, heavy lump at the edge of the bed.

While pouring a cup of coffee, I see Daisy out the window moving a wheelbarrow down our shared driveway but then the sight of her gets lost behind her overgrown garden. Even though she's out most mornings in her bohemian outfits, her long hair always in a braid running down her back, and those Crocs shoes that every gardener is required by law to own, I'm surprised to see her outside in the rain picking at weeds and pulling kale from her raised beds. She looks up just in time to see me peeking through the blinds and gives me a wave. I nod back and hope that she's not headed over to say hello. Although a very friendly woman, her empty nest has left a void for her. When she starts talking it's hard to find a break when you can excuse yourself, let alone add to the conversation. I have too much to do today and interacting with Daisy is just not on my list.

During my usual breakfast of oatmeal and black coffee I flip through the newspaper that's on the kitchen table before it's time to get to work studying for Mason's upcoming test. I have less than a week to understand such useful things as Dirichlet's Unit Theorem and regulators of an algebraic number field, and then it's on to more complicated ideas that will be beyond one person's capacity to keep in their head for any amount of time. Miranda always says that her brain is full, and she can't possibly remember one more thing. College seems to be an endless string of information. Every day new things are being told to you that you have to remember, things that you couldn't even imagine existed. It's like every idea they tell us is every person in China walking in a line that never ends because of the population increasing at such a steady rate.

Every time I open my notebook, I feel overwhelmed and I don't know where to start. I have a lot to review and there doesn't seem to be enough time to understand it all, or maybe my brain isn't capable of understanding. Why did I inflict this pain upon myself? Couldn't I have picked an easier major? Okay, c'mon Alice, you can do this.

After about an hour of studying, the rain has stopped and there's a rare glimpse of sunlight peeking through clouds, causing the wet grass to sparkle. I decide to sit on the back porch to get some fresh air and a little bit of relaxing peace, but I'm not ten feet from the house when I see Daisy dragging her wheelbarrow back to our adjoined garage.

"Alice, hey! Do you want some kale?" she inquires.

"No, thanks, we have some already," I inform her. No such luck avoiding her today as I originally planned.

"You didn't buy it at the store, did you? You know it's full of chemicals if it's not organic. Even then it's not one hundred percent safe. You really should plant your own or come over and grab some next time. I have so much, and I can't eat all of it. I always tell the neighbors to pick what they want, you know that. Oh

Alice, why didn't you just come over?"

I struggle for a reason that will suffice but instead just apologize because I won't be able to come up with an answer that is good enough.

"Did you meet the new neighbors?" Daisy asks.

"No, what new neighbors?" I try to engage, even though I'm not all that interested.

"The house on the corner, they finally sold it and the new owners moved in yesterday. Nice couple. He's in advertising and the wife is an engineer. They have a daughter who's ten. Sweet girl."

I don't know how she does it, but Daisy always knows everything about everybody in the neighborhood, even if they moved in yesterday. She likes to attend potlucks and organize block parties. There's always some event that she's inviting me to but for the most part, I have no interest. I'm just not as outgoing, and other than talking to Daisy, I barely know any of the neighbors. She says it's always good to know people in your neighborhood in case you need a cup of sugar, but I have never been so desperate for sugar that I couldn't walk to the corner store to get it.

Now that I'm all caught up on neighborhood events it's time to make my getaway. "Well, Daisy, it was good to see you, but I need to get back to work. I have a test next week."

"Oh Alice, you're gonna change the world someday. I'm so proud of you!" I immediately feel the burning sensation creep up on my cheeks when she says this, so I give her a wave and rush back inside. Daisy is always saying how proud of me she is, like I'm one of her daughters, except that one daughter dropped out of high school and the other is in California somewhere after she fell in love with an actor/poet/activist that convinced her to move to Los Angeles with him last year.

Once inside I see the red light flashing on my phone, letting me know that I missed a call from Cullen. His voicemail says he'll be coming home late tonight because they're having a retirement party for someone in his office. They're having drinks at *The Corral Pub* and he says he'll probably grab dinner while he's there. I guess I can stay in my sweatpants and t-shirt all day since I don't plan to go out, at least not past the backyard.

"C'mon Ricky, off my desk," I say to Rick Moranis who has settled in on top of my books. He can fall asleep anywhere, but it's usually the one place I need to be. When I open my laptop, I see that Miranda has sent me an article about a woman who teaches math through knitting. Oh good, there's a video too! This is mesmerizing. Leave it to Miranda to find a story like this. It keeps me entertained for a few minutes, but I know I need to focus. I write her back, "Clever, I love it," before I review the last chapter of notes I need to comprehend before the test.

I should create more structure in my day and make a plan to study at a certain time. That might help me to stay on track. I don't usually shower until late in the morning and some days it's after lunch. Today is no exception. After eating a large bowl of leftover chili, I shower and get dressed, but I feel like my productivity level is next to nothing. I don't have to be anywhere on my days off from school and even though I need to study, I don't have anyone expecting me to get my work done in a timely manner. By the time Cullen comes home from work, I'm on the couch but instead of watching TV like I usually am, I'm lost in a novel about a girl living in a foster home run by an eccentric woman who is trying to convince her to find Jesus.

"Hey hon," Cullen calls out as he walks in the front door. Meeting me on the couch, he kisses me and asks how my book is so far. I started it two days ago but I'm already halfway into it. I suppose if it's not a book detailing math proofs I can fly right through it.

"It's good. I read fifty pages tonight," I tell him.

"Nice! Did you have class today?"

"Nope, tomorrow. Miranda and I are meeting early to study for the test next week."

"Oh right, how's that class going?"

"It's okay. I mean, it's hard, but I think I'll make it. I worked for a few hours today on my homework and studied a little. I'll feel better after I go over it with Miranda."

"That's good. I'm sure you'll do great. You've been working hard," he says. After hearing Cullen's voice, Rick Moranis strolls out from the bedroom where he's been sleeping most of the day.

I roll my eyes. "I swear, he barely moves all day until he hears your voice, then he comes running," I complain, even though it's kind of a sweet trait for a cat to be happy to see his owner.

"Hey, buddy! How's my fat cat?" he asks.

"Don't say that to him...even though it's true." We try to keep him on a diet, but nothing seems to work. Cullen gives him a few rubs on the head before looking back at me. "I'm gonna go take a shower. Do you wanna finish that movie we rented?"

"Sure, that sounds great," I say and pick up my book to finish the chapter before he returns. When I'm done, I take a quick peek at the computer to find an email with the subject, "Students, open immediately." Oh no, that can't be good.

2

"We have to learn another new proof?" Miranda complained more than asked. She's sitting in the Brandford Hall study lounge which is so quiet today you can hear a pin drop.

"Oh yeah, you got Mason's email. I know, it's crazy. I don't know if I'll be able to learn that in time." Miranda and I are quickly getting our notebooks out to study but we're feeling a bit defeated. Professor Mason's email detailed a new proof that we have to learn and recreate on the upcoming test, which we're already stressed about. He liked to throw things at us at the last minute, so maybe we should have seen this coming.

"Do you wanna start with that?" I ask Miranda.

"I guess so. I looked at it last night but I'm having a hard time understanding it. What does this mean?" Miranda points to an unrecognizable symbol on the page.

"Let me see if it's in our notes." I flip through the pages from class and finally find what I'm looking for. "It's a complex conjugate isomorphism," I say with confidence but not entirely sure what it means.

"Oh right, I remember that now," Miranda replies with relief.

We already have a lot of studying to do today and having to learn an additional proof isn't helping our confidence level. I don't know why he's having us do this. We're only memorizing a proof and rewriting it exactly on the test, not interpreting its meaning or applying it in a practical way. I'm sure there's a logical reason for this, but it feels like a sadistic way of weeding out the weak students who are going to crack under the pressure.

It takes reciting the proof back and forth nearly twenty times before Miranda and I feel like we finally have it down. I can't say that I fully understand it, but I can recreate this on the test and feel that, for the most part, I know what I'm talking about. It's so helpful having a friend in this class. I'm not sure that I would have made it through without her support. Our study sessions go from supportive to venting, then somehow we end up feeling that we understand the material. It's great to talk this stuff out because it's hard to understand this all on my own. Miranda went from freaked out to only mildly freaked out, so that's a huge improvement, but I can tell that she's still worried.

"Are you feeling okay?" I ask her.

"I guess so. It's just that I study so much but it never feels like enough. Jacob and I are trying to plan the wedding, but I told him that I have to put it off for a while."

"Well, we only have a few months left. We'll get through it together," I tell her.

As more students start to arrive and settle in near us it becomes harder to concentrate. We spend nearly an hour and a half studying before I have to leave for my first class. Since the test isn't until Monday, we still have the weekend to keep working.

"Call me this weekend if you need any help," I tell Miranda before gathering my books. "Cullen has band practice on Sunday so you can even come over if you want to. The house will be quiet."

"Thanks, I'll let you know. By tomorrow this might all leave my brain. I don't think I can absorb anything new, so let's hope Mason doesn't send us any more emails. Unless it's to say that he's canceled the test and he's just gonna pass us all as a sign of goodwill."

"Yeah, don't hold your breath." I say. Luckily I only have one class today so I can get back home and at least attempt to study while this is all fresh in my head. This afternoon's class is Women's Studies 101 and since I actually enjoy that class, I should have an easy day. Fridays tend to be quieter since a lot of students tend to give themselves a three-day weekend around this time in the quarter. I try to stay proactive as long as I can, or I will easily fall behind. Today will be a nice dose of estrogen with a hint of cynicism about the patriarchy, so that will put me in a good mood for my afternoon of studying.

On the bus ride home, I practice reciting the

proof and only have to check my notes a few times when I get stuck. I must look like I'm reciting lines of a play. Every time I get stuck I wanna shout "Line!" to people sitting near me as if they have any idea what the next line is. There's a man who looks like he's in his fifties wearing an oversize red t-shirt sitting across from me. I'm not sure if he saw me studying the proof but he looks at my textbooks and asks if I'm coming from school.

"Yes, I go to Strauss University," I tell him.

"Oh, what are you studying?"

"Mathematics."

"Oh, wow!" he says surprised. "Are you gonna be a teacher?"

"No, I don't think so," I say, and he looks at me blankly.

"Hmm, so what are you gonna do then?" The man asks, completely dumbfounded by my interest in math without the inevitable goal of teaching.

"I'm not sure yet. I just know that I want to be a mathematician."

"Hmm. But what can you do with a degree in math?" he asks, even though I just gave him an answer.

"A lot of things. You can do almost anything; math is used in so many fields." This is usually my stock answer, but it's so vague and to be honest, I don't exactly feel it's a justified explanation.

"But you could teach, right?" he asks, repeating himself.

"Sure, but I don't plan to."

This answer still baffles him, but I just smile and

return to my studying, hoping to end the conversation. Thinking back, I've had some variation of this interaction multiple times since I decided to major in math. I think there's a belief that math is an antiquated subject that has no meaning other than to be taught, learned, and retaught on a pointless cycle without purpose. I wonder if male students get asked about becoming a teacher. People just assume it's what I'm gonna do. What if I had said I was studying biology? Would someone ask if I planned to be a biology teacher while the men became biologists? I should ask front-row-boy if he has to always explain his vocational plans to random strangers on the bus. I'm happy to see this man exit the bus a few minutes after we talk because he seemed to be disappointed in me by the tension I felt from his neighboring seat. I only have a few stops left myself, so I return to my studies and try to ignore this annoying line of questioning.

Walking through the front door I'm so grateful to see Rick Moranis greet me. He's looking a bit groggy but he's desperately in need of food, or so he proclaims when I walk into the kitchen.

"Okay, you win," I concede. I fill Rick Moranis's bowl and open the refrigerator to see that instead of anything edible there is an empty void. We haven't gone shopping in days and I'm in desperate need of sustenance if I'm gonna study for as long as I plan to. I suppose I could go to Daisy's garden and see what I can gather. Maybe I can make a salad for lunch. I think about that for a moment. "Yuck. Rick Moranis, I'd rather eat your food," I tell him. Also, if I go over to Daisy's I run the risk of getting locked into a thirty-minute conversation about spiritual enlightenment or the psychological power of aromatherapy. Nope, I don't have it in me today. Maybe I'll walk to Grant's Market and grab one of those takeout sandwiches I eat too often.

"Hey, Mr. Grant," I say, greeting my friendly acquaintance. Mr. Grant's oatmeal-colored sweater is matching his soft gray hair today. He's owned the corner market for fifteen years and I've seen him every time I've come in, except for one late evening when his niece had to fill in for him because his twelve-year-old Bloodhound went missing.

"Hi Alice, how's it going?" he replies.

"Good, thanks."

"Are you here for your usual? A *Loafing Around* sandwich?"

"Yes, there's nothing to eat in the house." I always hated the name of these sandwiches. Why do companies like puns so much? I just wish they didn't taste so good. I walk right to the back aisle, reach my hand into the refrigerated box, and pull out one of the last sandwiches on the shelf. I guess I'm not the only one who depends on these for survival.

"How's school going?" asks Mr. Grant from behind the counter.

"Pretty good. I have a test next week that I need to study for today. I'll be happy when this class is over. It's been pretty tough."

"Well, you're a bright girl. I'm sure you're gonna

24

do great."

"Thanks," I say, not convinced that is entirely true. I don't know if being 'a bright girl' is gonna get me through this time, but I take the compliment. It's nice to hear his confidence in me, even though being the owner of a corner store, Mr. Grant isn't an expert on my ability to pass a test. He has no idea about the amount of work I still need to do. "Have a great day," I tell him as he hands me my change.

"You too, Alice." It's a short walk home and I still have sixty-eight hours before this test. That should be plenty of time. Well, I guess if you subtract sleeping that's only forty-four hours. Also meals, that's more like thirty-seven hours. Still, plenty of time.

My backpack is still at the front door where I left it. I grab it and take out my notes, first trying to recite the proof I had just about mastered on the bus. It's been almost an hour and I still have it down. Success! Looking over the lecture notes and past homework assignments, I'm surprised that, overall, the material is making sense. My study session this morning with Miranda definitely helped. Maybe I don't need the next thirty-seven, no wait, thirty-six hours to study. Since I'm feeling so good, I decide it's time to reward myself with a little TV time and a snuggle with Rick Moranis.

Oh good, he's already on the couch waiting for me! Cullen calls when I'm halfway into a cooking show, making a mental note to make this meal, knowing of course that I probably never will.

"Hello love," I say, excited to hear his voice.

"Hey, you're in a good mood."

"Yep, I just finished my lunch and now I'm hanging out with Rick Moranis on the couch."

"That sounds fun," he says. "So, I'm gonna be home early tonight. Do you wanna go out for dinner?"

"Sure! Where were you thinking?" I ask, happy to be spending my Friday night going out with Cullen. We usually spend our Friday nights watching movies and getting takeout. This will be a nice alternative.

"Maybe that new Thai place?"

"Yeah, that sounds good. Miranda and Jacob went there last week. She said they really liked it."

"Okay, then it's a date. I should be home around six o'clock."

"Sounds good. I'll see you then. Love you."

"I love you too. Bye baby."

I should get back to work and study for a bit before Cullen comes home. Maybe I'll get a little dressed up for our date tonight. We haven't gone out in a while and it's nice not to be eating a dinner of Fritos in the library.

"I'll have the Pad See Ew," I say to the waitress and hand her my menu. Cullen is opting for the Drunken Noodles, an odd name but my second choice on the list of noodle dishes. Luckily we always end up sharing so I know I won't be disappointed that I didn't order it.

"So, you have your test on Monday?" he asks.

"Yeah," I reply.

"Still feeling good?"

"Yeah, pretty good. Miranda and I met this morning to study. She was a little freaked out about the proof we have to learn, but I think we both understand it now. I was studying a lot on the bus." I take a sip of water before remembering the unsolicited conversation I had today. "Oh! Some guy on the bus today was talking to me and when I told him I was majoring in math he asked if I wanted to be a teacher."

"Oh no, not another one." Cullen doesn't seem surprised by the interaction I had today because this isn't the first time I've told a story like this.

"I'm getting a little tired of this question. You know I have so much respect for teachers. This isn't me looking down on teachers, but I don't say that I'm majoring in Education. I just don't like how people always assume I want to teach. Just once I would love for someone to ask me about becoming a mathematician." In fact, this man on the bus brushed this career option aside so readily. He didn't even engage in the idea of my future as anything but a teacher.

"I know. It's frustrating." I can tell that Cullen is being supportive but already knows exactly what I'm gonna say. This rant happens far too often, so I try not to repeat what I have said so many times before.

"So, how was work today?" I ask, ready to change the subject.

"Good, I finished a huge project, so I'm glad that's over with. Dan called me into his office today. I was a little worried that there was a problem with the project, but he said I was getting a raise."

"Honey! That's awesome! You deserve it. You work so hard and it's about time they gave you a raise."

"It's no big deal," Cullen says, trying to be modest but I know he's proud of himself.

"Sure it is. Let's celebrate!" I catch the attention of our waitress. "Can we get a manhattan and a gin and tonic?" I look at Cullen. "It's on me."

"Thanks, but you didn't have to do that. It's just a small raise anyway."

"Yeah, but I'm happy for you. Anyway, it's good for us. I'm not working right now, and I know that's been hard."

"We're doing okay," he says. "Plus, you're gonna graduate in a couple of months and I know you've been looking for a job. You'll get something."

"I hope so."

"You can always teach," he says smirking.

"You know what, on second thought, I'm gonna sit at another table." Cullen laughs just as our waitress arrives with our drinks.

He raises his glass. "To you and your future as a mathematician," he says.

"Cheers! To you, not having to financially support your girlfriend for the rest of your life."

Forty-nine hours until the test. Still feeling good. I look at my phone to see a missed call from Miranda. "You have one new message," my friendly phone robot tells me.

"Hey Alice, it's me. I'm just calling to see if you

28

grabbed some of my notes by mistake. I can't find the handout for chapter three. Can you check and call me back?"

Oh no, I should have checked this sooner. She called last night when we were out for dinner, but I didn't see the call. I hop out of bed, rushing from the cold hardwood floor to the soft carpet to find my notebook still open on my desk in the living room. Shoot. Here's the handout she's looking for. How did I miss this yesterday?

"Alice?" The phone only rings once before Miranda picks up.

"Yeah, hey. Sorry I missed your call. I have the handout you're looking for. I must have stuck it in my notebook yesterday."

"Oh great!" she says, relieved. "Are you gonna be around later today? I could stop by in about an hour."

"Sure, I'll be here."

"Okay. See you soon," she says.

It's good that Miranda is coming over because it will give me an earlier start to the day. Most Saturdays I sleep in and Cullen and I watch TV for a while after breakfast. Since she's coming over in an hour that gives me enough time to take a quick shower. The warm water feels so relaxing, but I try not to linger too long. I'm gonna try to put on a pot of coffee before Cullen wakes up. By the time I make it back into the kitchen, I hear a knock at the door. Miranda is always showing up early and I shouldn't have expected today to be any different. Usually, when she gives me a time to meet her somewhere I try to show up ten minutes early to try to beat her there. It's never happened yet, but I keep hoping it will someday.

"Oh, Daisy. Hi," I say, trying not to seem too surprised to see her at my door.

"Good morning! You're not just waking up, are you?" Daisy has a habit of completing an entire day before I even start my first cup of coffee and she isn't shy about making me feel guilty about it.

"No, I've been up for a while. Showered and everything." I hope that my wet hair will convince her that I'm a productive member of society who doesn't sleep in on Saturdays, even though that would be perfectly acceptable, even expected of most people.

"That's good! You really shouldn't sleep too late. It's not healthy to be in bed for too long. Anyway, I was volunteering today at the library...you know I do the read-aloud there for the kids every Saturday? Well, I saw Luke and Melanie, the new neighbors. I told you about them the other day, remember? Well, they have a daughter, Kat. They said that they were looking for a math tutor for her. I told them you'd be perfect!"

"Oh, um, well, that's very nice but I'm really busy right now," I tell her, which is mostly true.

"Well, it wouldn't be that long I don't think. It would be a great experience for you, especially if you decide to teach." Here we go again.

"I'm not gonna be a teacher, Daisy, and besides, I have a big test coming up and I have to focus on my schoolwork."

30

"You should think about it. You'd be so great for her," Daisy says with an unconvincing smile. Before I can respond I see Miranda walking up the driveway.

"Hi," Miranda says softly, trying not to interrupt.

"Hey." I'm suddenly relieved that Miranda is early for everything. "Daisy, this is Miranda, Miranda this is my neighbor, Daisy." There's an awkward moment before I turn back to Daisy. "So, we have a lot of studying to do. I really should get going."

"Okay, but think about it won't you?" Daisy asks. I give her a nod and rush Miranda inside.

"What was that all about?" Miranda asks.

"Oh, nothing. Someone's looking for a tutor."

"Cool. Who is it?"

"Our new neighbor. Their daughter is ten. What is that, fifth grade?"

"But you hate kids."

"No, I don't," I say, a little offended.

"Oh, sorry, I just never heard you say anything good about kids. Maybe I assumed."

"Well, it's not that. I just need to focus on my schoolwork right now. Besides, we have this test on Monday and I need to get through Mason's class. You know that."

"I know, but it might be a good experience."

Miranda is always thinking that the universe is sending us good experiences. "That's what Daisy said too," I inform her. "I just don't have the time right now."

"Well, can I get that handout? I should get back

and study a little more." Following me into the living room, Miranda and I retrieve what she is looking for.

"Hey, Rick Moranis." Miranda reaches down to pet him on the head. "That always makes me laugh! Who names their cat Rick Moranis? You guys are so weird."

As Miranda heads out I see Daisy in her front yard and quickly shut the door. I don't want to continue the conversation with her because she'll end up talking me into taking that job. I swear she's always pushing me to do things like this. She assumes we all want to be involved in each other's lives and help our neighbors. Daisy has a very "it takes a village" attitude. She thinks that we should all be part of some grand commune where we teach each other's kids about life...or at least about math. I wish she didn't tell them I'd be a good tutor for them. I mean, I appreciate her saying so, I guess, but she just doesn't understand the pressure I'm under.

When Cullen comes out of the bedroom Rick Moranis runs over to see if he can get a little attention from his favorite head-scratcher. I'm in the kitchen filling the coffee pot, trying not to be annoyed by Daisy's persistence.

"Hey, little boy." He falls for that cute little face every time. As he bends down to get to the perfect head-scratching level, he asks, "Was someone just here?"

"Yeah, Miranda. I accidentally took a part of her notes that she needed. She came to pick it up."

"Oh, okay, I thought I heard Daisy."

"Yeah, she was here too. She came over to tell

me that she ran into the new neighbors at the library this morning."

"Seriously? Who's up that early on a Saturday?"

"I know, right? She volunteers there. Anyway, she said the new neighbors have a daughter and they're looking for a math tutor," I say, trying to be informative instead of complaining.

"Oh no, let me guess. Did she volunteer you?" Cullen asks, already knowing the answer.

"Pretty much," I reply. He knows Daisy all too well.

"Are you gonna do it?"

"I don't think so. I'm too busy right now. Speaking of which, I should probably study."

"Well, I'll be on the couch if you need me," he says and turns to his furry friend. "C'mon Rick Moranis."

3

I woke up before my alarm today, which rarely happens. The calm energy I felt over the weekend has now turned into anxiety. Three hours until my test. I'm still feeling...good?

Cullen left for work early this morning but was nice enough to make me a pot of much-needed coffee. "Good luck on your test. Call me when you're done. I love you," reads the note he left on the counter. I smile, pouring myself a cup.

I never felt anxious about taking tests until this year. Mason's class is so hard, and even though Miranda and I study and do all the homework, I'm not completely getting it all. I was actually a little fearful of taking a class with Professor Mason to begin with. He didn't have the best reputation on campus, but all the other classes I needed were full by the time I registered.

Thank goodness Cullen made coffee this morning. He brews it strong and it's dark and bitter and delicious. It's nice to have a moment to relax this morning and take a little extra time to clear my head. It's eerily quiet outside except for the steady taps of rain hitting the windows. I don't want to look at my notes anymore because I'm afraid I'll catch something I didn't see before and start to worry that I don't know as much as I think I do. It feels like all the math inside my brain is going to bust out if I try to make room for more information. Right now I'm feeling confident and calm knowing that I did as much as I could to prepare. It seems like every spare moment this weekend I was reciting the proof, so I should have it down by now. I'm ready for the test but anxious to get it over with.

It's good that I'm up early so I don't have to rush. There's nothing worse on a test day than feeling stressed about being late. I leave the house so early that I make it to the bus stop with plenty of time to spare. No bus delays today, which is good. I often take the earlier bus in case, and today was no exception. I don't want to have to rush to class because of construction or, believe it or not, geese crossing the road. It happened once and although it was a long wait, the driver threw up his hands in defeat and burst out laughing.

Looking around the bus today, most travelers are covered in rain gear. When it comes to outerwear, people are usually more prepared than I am, which is evident today by my lack of proper attire. I pause to look out the window and see rain falling in huge drops on the sidewalk, unlike when I left for the bus this morning when there was only a drizzle.

A woman with a bright pink umbrella is waiting at the next stop. After she gets on the bus, she folds her vinyl contraption and digs in her change purse for the bus fare. Once she finds a seat, she immediately grabs what appears to be a muffin from her oversize bag. It's most likely the same bag Mary Poppins pulled a lamp out of.

When I get off the bus, I make a run for it, trying to hide under canopies along the storefront windows. Others are doing the same and it's hard to avoid bumping into pedestrians on my way to class. Ahead of me I notice a guy from my class who holds the door open to our building entrance so I can run inside. I take a moment just inside the doorway so I can shake out my wet hair and catch my breath.

In the hallway, Miranda is sitting on one of the benches where we often wait for Professor Mason to arrive. When I see him walking down the hallway a few moments later, I notice he's holding a handful of folders with a paper coffee cup balancing on top. Entering our classroom, students immediately take out their notes to study. There are only a few spare minutes left and I can almost feel the tension in the air. I overhear a handful of guys talking about overly complex concepts from another class. Apparently, they are trying to show us that they are not at all worried about the next seventy-five minutes of their lives.

"Okay class, put everything away. You'll need a calculator and a pencil and that's it. I don't want to see any notebooks on the table. Put everything under your chairs. Eyes on your own paper. You have the entire class to work." Professor Mason is almost chipper this morning. Almost.

The packet of questions hits my desk with a thud. Flipping through, there are four pages and twelve questions in all. I start with the proof I need to get out of my brain before I completely forget everything I practiced, then I flip back to the front page. Oh no. I don't know how to answer the first question. I'll skip to the next one. Oh no, no, no. As I look over the test, I realize that this is going to be much harder than I thought. Sixty-two minutes left and my confidence is slipping away. Oh no. Oh no.

The clock is ticking like a metronome and I can hear audible sighs coming from a guy across the room. This oddly breaks the tension because it's so ridiculous that it makes me laugh to myself. As much as I would like to join him in his frustrated sounds, I continue to push through and answer as many questions as I can make sense of. As soon as the first person rises from their desk to hand in their test I start to panic. Surprisingly, Miranda is the third person done and when I see her walking her test up to Mason's desk, I really get worried. Is she done already? How did she do this? I'm only halfway. Focus. Focus. Head down, you can do this.

With only three minutes to spare I managed to write at least the essence of an answer to every question. When I bring my test up to Professor Mason's desk, I give him a fake smile and say "thank you" as I hand him my test. "Thank you"? What am I thanking him for? You made a test that stressed me out for the last seventy-two minutes. Now I'm worried that I have no idea what is going on in class. Yes, thank you so much.

Miranda is outside the classroom waiting for me when I finally emerge. "How'd you do?" she asks impatiently.

"Not great."

"Oh, I'm sure you did okay. I probably failed it."

"Yeah right. You were one of the first ones done," I tell her, annoyed that she's always so self-deprecating.

"I know, but I skipped the last two questions."

"Well, I hope we'll find out next class. I don't want to wait until next week to find out that I failed. Mason needs a TA. He takes forever to grade our tests," I say, but I'm not actually looking forward to finding out how I did. Miranda walks me to the coffee cart before heading to her next class and as soon as I give my drink order I give Cullen a call.

"Hey baby." His voice is quiet. I can always tell if he's busy at work by the volume of his voice.

"Hey," I reply.

"Uh oh, what's wrong? How did your test go?"

"Not great," I tell him.

He tries to be reassuring. "I'm sure it's not that bad."

"Oh, are you *sure*?" My voice is low and he can tell that I'm disappointed.

"Okay, I'm not sure, but maybe it's not as bad as you think."

"Maybe." Even though I called for support, it's easier to be negative. Perhaps I'm just as self-deprecating as Miranda.

"Are you done for the day?" he asks.

"Yes, I'm done with classes anyway."

"Do you wanna grab a cup of coffee?" Cullen works a few blocks away and meeting for coffee is a great excuse for him to get out of the office for a while.

"No, that's okay. I'm at the coffee cart now. I'm just gonna grab something and head home."

"Alright, well, I have to work late again. I should be home by seven o'clock. Possibly seven-thirty."

"Tacos tonight?" I ask, giving myself something to look forward to.

"Sounds good"

"Okay, see you tonight. I love you."

"Love you too."

My coffee is nearly cold by the time I get to the bus stop, but this is the least of my worries. I keep replaying the test over and over again. Even if the correct answers come to me, it's too late. The test is in Mason's hands now and I can just hope that everyone else does so poorly that he curves the grades. He's usually not that generous but anything's possible. Walking onto the bus I try to force myself to think about something other than the test, but I'm unable to come up with any other thoughts.

The rain has stopped by the time I get off the bus so at least I don't have to get drenched again. As I turn the corner towards the house, I see Daisy talking to a woman down the street who I assume is the new neighbor. I'm sure Daisy ambushed the poor woman as soon as she saw her returning from wherever she's coming from. Grocery shopping, I assume from the brown bags inside of the open car trunk.

"Alice! Hi, I'm so glad to see you!" Daisy shouts as soon as she notices me. Man, I'm not in first impression mode right now. She waves me over with such excitement at the luck of running into me. Right, luck. I'm ten yards from my house and walking down the street like I do every single Monday morning at the exact same time. She must have planned this.

"Alice, this is Melanie," she says when I approach. "We were just talking about you, go figure." Yep, go figure.

"Hi Melanie, how are you?" I ask, trying to be neighborly.

"Good thanks, it's nice to meet you. Daisy says you're studying math at Strauss University. That's very exciting."

"Yeah, it can be," I reply. I suppose it can be exciting on days when I haven't bombed a test that I spent hours preparing for.

"I was telling Melanie that you were thinking about the tutoring job," Daisy informs me.

I shoot her a look but try to be polite. "Um, yeah, I might be able to, but I'm pretty busy right now. School and everything."

"Sure, right, but you could probably do it. It wouldn't be that much time, right Melanie?" Daisy looks at her with a smile, but I can tell that Melanie can feel Daisy pressuring me.

41

"Maybe just a few sessions? But if you're busy we understand," Melanie says, trying to shield me from Daisy's persistence.

"Yeah, I'm sorry. I can't right now. Maybe when I'm done with this class? I'm planning to graduate in the spring and I'm under a lot of pressure."

"Oh, of course. No worries."

I can tell that Daisy is annoyed with me but I'm not in the mood. Adding on extra work is about the last thing I need right now. I'm sure I won't be hearing the end of this, but I have to get out of here.

"I should get going. It was nice to meet you," I tell Melanie, trying to avoid looking in Daisy's direction.

"You too," Melanie says.

Walking into the house I want to draw all the blinds closed and hide. I'm feeling defeated by my poor performance on the test and annoyed at the world. "Ugh, I told Daisy I was too busy. Why does she always put me in that position? I'm sure Melanie thinks I'm a flake, even though I never said yes in the first place," I say to Rick Moranis. He looks up at me with his large cat eyes, confused. Before I can get into my sweatpants, which I plan to live in for the rest of the day, Miranda sends me a text. "Chin up, we got this. Call me if you want to vent." She has a great way of keeping me motivated, even when I'm feeling at my worst. It's nice to have a friend through all this who understands the pressure. I feel like I not only have to do as well as the guys, but I have to do better. I don't want anyone saying, "See, she's a girl. She can't do math. I knew it all along."

I'm relieved there's leftover pizza in the fridge from last night and I don't have to worry about leaving the house. What can I binge-watch on TV to make me feel better? Oh, right, that true-crime documentary about the guy who was framed for murder with his nephew. That can easily take up the rest of my day. I'll watch this before Cullen comes home from work because he's not a fan of all the melodramatic nonsense. I, on the other hand, am riveted.

PLUNK. Cullen's bag hits the floor in the kitchen as Rick Moranis jumps off my lap in the most ungraceful fashion.

"Hey honey," I call out.

"Hi, sweetheart, what are you up to?"

"Oh, just watching something stupid on TV," I inform him.

He smiles. "Don't tell me, a true-crime show?"

"Yes, that documentary I was watching last week," I say, slightly embarrassed by my time spent on the couch all day. "Do you want me to start making the tacos?" I ask in order to seem productive.

"Sure, I'll help in a minute once I get out of my work clothes."

We started having a weekly taco night a few months back and I've come to enjoy it. We go all out and we even make our own guacamole and handmade tortillas. We couldn't keep buying the packaged nonsense they try to pass off in the store as "authentic" once we realized how much better the real thing was.

43

"How was work today?" I ask Cullen when he arrives back in the kitchen.

"Good, pretty normal." Cullen grabs some items from the pantry as I take out the tortilla dough from the fridge. "I was in the office most of the day. Matt was having some issues with his project, so I spent a lot of time helping him. He's been there for six months and he's still not getting it."

"Well, not everyone can be a genius like you," I say with a smirk.

"No, that's true," he replies with no hint of sarcasm. "So, what happened with your test?"

"I dunno," I say, pressing the dough into flat little pancakes and piling them into a small, neat stack. "It was harder than I thought it was gonna be. I did the proof no problem, but the rest was really confusing."

"How did Miranda do?"

"She says she skipped the last two problems and thinks she failed it, but I bet she got an A. She studied so much."

"Well, so did you," he says. "When do you find out your grade?"

"Hopefully on Wednesday," I tell him.

"Try not to worry too much. You've done well in that class so far. I don't think it's gonna be so bad."

"I hope not." I try to believe him, but it's hard not to feel a little bit defeated. It's good to talk to Cullen and making dinner together is a nice distraction. I'm glad I have someone to unwind with at the end of the day. I can get in my own head and I have a hard time compartmentalizing and putting things in perspective. This is only one test. Even if I don't do well, I know the rest of my grades in Mason's class are good enough to keep me going. I'm gonna try not to obsess over this for the next few days.

Before class on Wednesday morning, I overhear some students talking about the last problem on the test as they try to compare answers. Miranda and I look at each other because we can relate to their worries. It seems like a lot of students had the same struggle we did. I fear that we won't know how we did for at least another seventy-five minutes of staring at the clock. Professor Mason has a habit of returning tests at the end of class. He doesn't want us spending the whole class period thinking about our grades. When he arrives in class, I can see a pile of not-so-neatly stacked papers in a folder. I assume my fate is in there somewhere.

As predicted, Mason starts the lecture without handing back our tests. "You can pick up your tests today on the way out," Mason announces. "For the most part, the class did pretty well, except for question twelve and I will share the solution on the class message board."

Miranda turns to me with a look of relief on her face. "At least I wasn't the only one who couldn't do that one," she whispers.

"Yeah, that makes me feel a little better," I tell her.

Waiting an entire class period is torture. I can't

focus at all on the lecture, which is having the opposite effect that Mason tried to achieve. Not knowing is worse than seeing how poorly I did. I look at the clock over and over but only a minute has passed in between glances. When the class is finally over, Miranda and I wait for the crowd of students to disperse before we head to the front. I don't quite know what to expect. Some students look relieved, while some are rushing out the door without even looking at their scores. When there are only a few students left, Miranda and I walk up together to look through the remaining papers left in the stack. I'm a little afraid to look but I turn to the back page where I know my grade is waiting for me. My eyes stare blankly at the page because I don't believe what I'm seeing.

"Wait, what? This is impossible," I tell Miranda.

4

I passed? How did I pass? I look over my test in disbelief. Mason's comments are a little vague and there are red pen marks all over the place, but I passed! I look over at Miranda who doesn't seem as pleased as I am.

"How'd you do?" I ask her.

"Failed. Oh my god, I failed." Miranda is flipping through each page over and over again, trying to see if the results will change. Or possibly she's hoping the grade will magically disappear like shaking an Etch-A-Sketch.

"Oh no. I'm sorry Miranda."

"Man, I can't believe I failed. I thought maybe he wouldn't count the last question since everyone did so bad on it. Failed. I can't believe it. I....failed."

"That sucks. I'm really sorry, Miranda. At least the rest of your grades in class are good. You'll probably be okay. It's just one grade." It's easy to say this now that I passed but, if our roles were reversed, I'd be just as devastated as she is.

"You passed, didn't you?" Miranda asks, not

exactly wanting to hear the answer.

"Yes. I don't know how."

Miranda is still looking over her test paper and doesn't look up. "Well, congrats," she says. "At least one of us passed. Man, I'm gonna have to work so hard now to keep my grade up."

"I know, hang in there. We'll get through it." I try to be supportive just like Miranda has been for me in the past. This hasn't been an easy journey, but we've always helped each other. "How about I buy you a cup of coffee? Or one of those caramel latte things you like so much? With whipped cream? Extra whipped cream?" I'm hoping a sugar rush will help to alleviate the pain.

"Sure. That sounds good."

At the coffee cart I try to talk about happier things, but Miranda is too bummed about her grade. I try not to show it but I'm so relieved that I passed. I was preparing myself for the worst all weekend and all through class I thought for sure that I would be upset the rest of the day. I can imagine how worried Miranda must be, but as soon as she's out of earshot I can't help myself. I have to call Cullen right away and share the good news.

"Guess what? I passed!" I tell Cullen over the phone, not being able to wait for him to guess.

"That's awesome! I knew you would! See, all that worrying for nothing."

"I know, I know. I couldn't believe it. Miranda failed though." I change my voice to a more sympathetic tone. "She's taking it pretty hard," I inform him.

"Oh man, that's too bad."

"Yeah, but I think she'll bounce back. We just have a few more assignments and then the final exam, and she's done pretty well so far. Mason is so hard though. I can't wait for this class to be over with."

"I know, it seems like it's been a tough one."

"Tough is an understatement!"

When I hang up with Cullen, I see front-row-boy passing by with his infamously messy hair and just-got-out-of-bed look. Sometimes I think it takes effort to look this disheveled. I really want to ask him how he did on the test, but I've never talked to him even once. Miranda and I have reenacted a few moments in class with me playing the role of Professor Mason and Miranda starring in the key role of front-row-boy, asking question after question, but her acting was a bit over the top. I may not be able to get that image out of my head if I actually talked to him at this moment, so I continue on my way, knowing that at least I did well and that's what matters.

I'm feeling bad for Miranda though. I know she studied really hard. She must be feeling pretty down on herself. It's really easy to get upset about our grades. We work so much and try so hard, but sometimes it doesn't feel like enough.

When I get on the bus, I think about calling her, but by the time I get on, I decide to relax and take comfort in knowing that this test is behind me. Just one quarter left, then this will all be over. All the stress of college will be in the past. I should really be focusing on what's to come next and make a plan for after college. I've been looking at internships, but nothing seems right.

At the front of the bus, a man is making goofy faces at a little girl with bows in her hair. She's maybe three years old, although I've never been good at telling how old kids are. She might be one, or six. I have no idea. Her mom is smiling back and forth at them and the girl is now giggling in high-pitched little shrieks. She seems so happy and it makes me smile. She's so innocent without a care in the world, so happy to get the attention. It's nice that even a routine bus ride has its moments.

Oh shoot, I just remembered I have to stop by the market today. I should do that on the way home. It's a warm, teaser day that makes you think that winter is finally over even though we still have months of dreary rainy days ahead. The short walk is a pleasant one as I'm warmed by the rare appearance of the sun. I'm paying so much attention to the unseasonably warm weather that when I open the entrance doors I almost run smack into Melanie.

"Oh, hi, Melanie. It's Alice. We met the other day," I say to her, scrambling to recover from our near collision.

"Yes of course. How are you?"

"Good, really good," I tell her. "How about you?"

"Not bad," she says, adjusting a large grocery bag that is slipping out of her arm.

I'm not one for small talk but I try to be friendly since I wasn't being my best self during our first

50

encounter. "Are you guys all moved in?" I ask.

"Just about. I don't like to live out of boxes for too long, so we're mostly unpacked," she tells me.

"Yeah, I'm the same way."

"Have you lived in this neighborhood long?"

"About a year. My boyfriend and I used to live on the other side of the river, but we were just renting then. I wanted to buy a house which was a really tough process. It's a seller's market. Well, you probably know that."

"Oh boy do we ever. Actually, I think I saw him the other morning," Melanie says.

"Who? Oh, right. Cullen, yeah, he mentioned that he saw you too." I realize I'm still holding the door open and two girls awkwardly walk between us trying to get inside.

"Well, I should probably go. It was nice seeing you, Melanie."

"Yeah, you too. Have a nice day," she says with a little wave.

Inside the market, I notice that the two girls I held the door for are dressed in school uniforms. I can't believe they have to wear saddle shoes. Do they even still make saddle shoes? I think the girls are in high school, but again, I can't tell ages of anyone from toddlers to teens.

"Do you have any fabric softener?" one girl calls out to Mr. Grant who is helping an older woman at the checkout. This seems like an incredibly odd question coming from a high school girl. What era are these girls from?

"No, we're all out right now," Mr. Grant calls back to them.

They look at each other. The girl who asked about the fabric softener sighs to the other in disappointment and they walk out without purchasing anything. I place my non-domestic items on the counter. "That was a strange request, don't you think?" I ask Mr. Grant.

"Oh, that was Erin Hayes. She's taking care of her grandmother," he tells me.

"Do you mean Mrs. Hayes, the science teacher from Dunmore Elementary?"

"Yes, she's been sick for a while and Erin and her family have been looking after her."

"Oh wow, I had no idea. Mrs. Hayes was my teacher. I always loved her." Thinking of her for the first time in years I remember something odd about her. "She never wore shoes, never. Even in the winter she would stroll the halls in socks. I don't know how they let her do that," I tell him.

"Yeah, she's an eccentric. She lived in New York City and hung out with Andy Warhol in the '80s."

"Really? That's incredible," I say, amazed. "I should tell my friend Miranda. She was obsessed with Warhol when she was at art school. She'll be so jealous. I'm sorry to hear that Mrs. Hayes is sick though."

"Yeah, she's a sweet lady," Mr. Grant adds. I wish him a good day and head back out into the warmth of the afternoon.

After I text Miranda to tell her about my two degrees of separation from Andy Warhol, I start to think about Mrs. Hayes and what a great teacher she was. She made her class so fun and I learned so much. I didn't even feel like I was in a classroom. I felt like we were actual scientists the way she got us engaged in the lessons. It's sweet that her granddaughter is taking care of her. I'm not sure who will take care of me in my old age. Cullen possibly, but he'll be as old as I am. Rick Moranis surely isn't going to make it that long and even if he did, he's basically useless as a caretaker.

"The Beatles? How is that supposed to be The Beatles?" I ask Miranda who has done a very poor job of acting out the iconic band. Miranda and Jacob have invited us over for a Friday game night, which usually results in an embarrassing game of charades where the boys beat us every time.

"I was walking down Abbey Road," she says, exasperated.

I laugh. "That made no sense," I tell her.

"Well, I was. You just didn't get it," she tells me.

It's nice to be laughing and blowing off some steam. We haven't had a game night in a long time. The guys usually end up talking about music since Jacob is a drummer. He hasn't played in a band for six months, but he still drums in his spare time. Miranda and I try not to talk about class too much, but it doesn't always work out. She's still worried about her grade but seems to be more positive than when I left her a few days ago.

"Two words. Movie. First word. Driving, car, parking a car, driving in a car, truck driver..." Cullen tries to understand what Jacob is acting out. This is looking good. It seems like we actually have a chance at winning tonight.

I turn to Miranda. "Are you guys still planning to go to Bali for your honeymoon?" I ask.

"Yeah, we want to. Jacob's sous chef went there for his honeymoon and said it was incredible." Miranda opens another bottle of wine and reaches out to fill my glass. "What about you guys? Any wedding bells in your future?"

"No, we don't plan to get married. We've talked about it, but we're happy the way things are."

"Plus, you don't want kids anyway," Miranda adds.

"Yeah, that's true," I say, although it seems like an odd point for Miranda to make. "I don't see the need to get married. No offense! It's just not for us."

"That's okay. I didn't think I was gonna get married until I met Jacob. When he proposed I was shocked, right? But I said yes right away. I could see myself married to him, ya know?"

"Yeah, you were shocked for some reason, but we all saw it coming. We knew you guys would end up getting married."

"Oh no, is this wedding talk?" Cullen asks, hoping to avoid any more wedding planning conversations. They have unsuccessfully acted out *Rearview Mirror* and Miranda and I take the lead for the first time in the history of charades.

"Changing the subject now. Jacob, how's work going?" I ask.

Jacob hands Cullen a beer and sits in a paisley print chair they found at a thrift store last month. "It's good. We've been a little slow lately. We usually die down a bit this time of year," he tells me.

"That makes sense. We don't usually go out that much when it rains like this." I say, commenting on the return of cold winter weather.

"Although last week we went to that new Thai place," Cullen says. I can tell he's trying to make it seem like we're still a fun, young couple that goes out on Friday nights.

"It turned into a bit of a celebration actually because Cullen got a raise at work."

"Congrats, man," Jacob raises his beer. "Cheers."

"Cheers!" Miranda and I add in unison, clinking our glasses together. The joyful support only lasts a moment, however. It's time to get down to business. I pick up our next card, unable to hide my satisfaction. "Okay, Miranda. We've got this."

Cleaning up our scattered game pieces and nearly empty bowls of food on the coffee table after our victory, I ask Miranda how she's feeling about Mason's class.

"Fine, I guess," she says. "I'm worried about the test grade, but I should be okay."

"I can't believe we only have one quarter left. It

seems like we just met, doesn't it?" I ask, reminiscing.

"Yeah, in some ways. But I also feel like I've been in school forever. I'm ready to move on."

"Me too," I tell her. "It's scary though. We have to leave the protective halls of the school and look for real jobs."

"I know, I'm a little worried, but I'm sure we'll find something. There are so many jobs out there." She grabs some cards that had fallen to the floor and adds them neatly to the rest of the pile. "Hey, whatever happened with that tutoring job? Your neighbor was looking for someone?"

"Oh, I told them I was too busy."

"That's too bad."

"Yeah, it's just not a good fit for me right now. Daisy is probably annoyed with me," I tell her.

"How come?"

"Because she thought for sure I would do it. She likes to help everyone, which is sweet, but she practically accepted the job on my behalf before she even talked to me."

"She must think highly of you," Miranda says.

"I know, but she just gets so excited. Maybe some other time."

The guys are wrapping up what seems to be an endless conversation about some local band that Jacob saw last month. "You should totally check them out," he informs Cullen. "The guitarist is insane. Really, you should come next time."

"Yeah, let me know," Cullen says.

"Maybe the girls should come too," Jacob adds.

Miranda and I look at each other. "I think we'll be too busy for a while," I tell him.

It's great that the guys get along so well. That isn't always the case with friends, but Miranda and Jacob are very similar to us. It's weird to have met another math girl and her musician boyfriend. It's like meeting another unicorn who also lives with a leprechaun.

"Let's do this again sometime," Miranda says and hands me a container full of Jacob's homemade apple fritters for the road. "This was really fun."

"Definitely," I say as I'm pulling on my rain boots. "It's nice to take a break for a while."

Outside the streets are quiet and there's a sweet smell of rain. The neighbors across the street must be watching TV because there's a flickering light shining through the curtains. Even though the car is cold, I feel warmth when I get in and smile at Cullen.

"Apple fritter, my love?"

"Don't mind if I do."

5

One more week and we're done with Mason's class. Miranda recovered from her test grade and has been working like mad, studying almost every night. We've been meeting before class once a week to review the lecture notes and help each other with any homework questions we're struggling with.

"Are you still gonna register for next quarter's classes this afternoon?" she asks.

"Yes, I have a break before my second class, so I should be able to meet with our advisor."

"Well, try to get Jane Freeman for Number Theory. I hear she's amazing." Jane Freeman is new to Strauss University. She's finishing her PhD and we have been hearing a lot of students raving about her. "She teaches the Monday/Wednesday class. We can sign up together." Miranda's voice lowers a bit. "If we pass this class, that is."

"We're gonna pass. Look how much work we've done! No one is working this hard in our class, I swear. Don't worry." I don't actually know if that's true, but it feels like we've been studying nonstop, so I can't imagine anyone else is working harder than we are.

Through the crowd in the hallway, I see front-row-boy walking towards us. "Look," I say to Miranda, motioning in his direction. "It looks like he might have showered today."

"Doubtful. But he looks like he bought a hairbrush, so that's an improvement."

"I hope he ends up interviewing for the same jobs we do," I say. "We'll get hired over him no problem!"

"Maybe he gets all dressed up in his normal life. Like, when he gets home he changes into a suit or something."

Laughing I try to imagine him in a suit, all dressed up and ready for a night in on the couch. "Nope, not possible."

Students in the hallway are starting to get up and walk to our classroom door. "Looks like Professor Mason is coming," Miranda notices.

We gather our possessions and head into class looking for a new place to sit. We have been trying to change our seats from the back row, but most students sit in the same place every class, even though they're not assigned. We boldly make our way to the front where a few seats are empty, and Miranda gets out her stack of infamous colored pens.

"Okay class, settle in. Today we're gonna wrap up chapter five and then you're gonna break into groups to work on the final exam review handout I gave you," says Professor Mason. "That will be a good time to ask me any questions you have about the final next week."

Miranda and I look at each other with both hope and dread in our eyes. The last few weeks of class have gone pretty smoothly and with all of our time spent studying, we're feeling positive about the upcoming final.

After lecturing for twenty-five minutes, Professor Mason breaks us into study groups. Other than working with Miranda, I actually prefer to work on my own. Study groups aren't always productive. They often turn into talk about other classes or things happening on campus.

Mason calls out our assigned study partners. "You four are a group, you five, this row is a group, and one, two, three, four of you in the back." Oh no, why did we sit in the front today? Front-row-boy is in our group and when I turn to Miranda, she already has an annoyed look on her face. We reluctantly pull our desks together hoping that if we go slow enough Mason will change his mind and let us work alone.

We're quiet for a few moments and I'm the first to speak. "Hey, it's Andy, right?" I ask one of the group members.

"Yes," he replies.

"I'm Alice, this is Miranda."

"Charlie," mutters front-row-boy. "Do you guys wanna jump right in or work alone for a bit?"

Andy doesn't hesitate. "Let's jump right in. One and two look pretty straight-forward so we can skip those. Number three uses the Dirichlet Unit Theorem, but we should talk about number four. That proof looks like the one on last week's assignment. What do you think, Charlie?"

Is this guy for real? He's barely looking at either me or Miranda and just dictated our entire study session. I actually have a few questions about number one, but we're already past that. Determined, I turn to Miranda. "What do you think about number one?"

"That one's really easy," interrupts Charlie.

"Well, I still would like to go over it," I tell him, confident but annoyed.

"You just have to use L'Hôpital's Rule to find the limit," he explains with a sigh.

"Okay, great. Well, I'm gonna work on that, but you guys can feel free to move ahead," I say. "I'd like to work at my own pace."

"Me too," says Miranda without hesitation. She always has my back and I know she doesn't want to follow their lead out of solidarity with me. We can tell that these guys aren't thrilled to work with us but we're not gonna let them run this thing. By the time I get to number six, I hear Andy and Charlie talking about a party in the dorms last night. Andy is halfway through describing a drunken argument between his buddy and another guy on their floor when I interrupt.

"Number six is pretty easy but what did you guys get for number seven?" I ask.

They look down at the page and back to me. "Oh, we're not there yet," Charlie says. By the look on his face, he must have thought that Miranda and I would take a long time to complete our work and he would have a lot of time to waste.

"Well, let me know when you get there," I say with a smile.

This situation is so uncomfortable that I start to pack my things before we're dismissed from class so I can make my getaway. As soon as Mason releases us for the day, Miranda and I drag our desks back to their original positions in the row and bolt out the door. I'm so annoyed at Andy and Charlie and their attitude. Miranda and I work so well together, but I didn't feel very productive in our forced study group.

"Well, that was fun." Miranda's voice is dripping with sarcasm and I can tell by her tone that she's just as irritated as I am.

"Yeah, a blast. What's with them?"

"I don't know, but let's agree never to sit in the front row again."

"Agreed."

As I turn the corner walking home from the bus, I notice a young girl poking around Daisy's garden beds. She has a short, funky haircut with green streaks in her bangs. I see her pulling out some carrots when I get closer to her.

"Hi there," I say to her.

"Um, hi," she says nervously. "Daisy said I could take some carrots if I wanted them. She said she has a lot and doesn't want them to go to waste."

"Sure, that makes sense. She's really good about sharing with the neighbors." I try to reassure her that she's not doing anything wrong. "Do you live nearby?"

"Yes. I live right there," she says, pointing to the brick house on the corner with a green bike resting on the front porch.

"Oh, you must be Kat. I met your mom a while back." Kat continues to dig through the soil, pushing away worms and shaking debris off the leafy tops after the carrots emerge from the ground. "Is that your bike? You must like green," I say, pointing to her hair.

"Yes, it's my favorite color." She continues to dig. "It's called *Luck of the Irish*."

"What is?"

"My hair color. My mom did it for me."

"Well, I like it very much." After another minute of digging, Kat stands up to brush the wet grass from the knees of her black overalls. "I like your shoes," I say, pointing to her green Converse sneakers that I didn't notice before. I look down at my own, now faded and dingy, the yellow not as bright as it once was.

"Cool. I like yours too."

"I'm Alice, by the way."

"Hi, Alice." Kat finally meets my eye line. "I should get home now."

"Of course. I'll see you around, Kat." She grabs the carrots that she pulled from the ground, making sure to brush back the displaced soil around the edges of the garden beds.

"Bye. Can you tell Daisy thanks for the carrots?"

64

"Absolutely," I say as I give her a wave goodbye.

Turning towards my side of the driveway, I see Cullen on the front porch collecting the mail. "Who was that you were talking to?" He pulls a small stack of envelopes from the mailbox and opens the door for me, following me inside.

"Kat. She's the daughter of the new neighbors. Well, the neighbors that moved in last month. Remember, I met her mom, Melanie?"

"Oh, right. The girl that needed a math tutor."

"Yep. She's really cool. She has green Converse sneakers."

"Nice! It sounds like a perfect match." Cullen is flipping through a guitar magazine. "How was class today?"

"Fine, I guess. We finished the new material for the quarter but then we had to work in groups to review for the final. Wanna guess who was in my group?"

"Don't tell me..." he says, trailing off.

"Yep, front-row-boy. Well, actually, his name is Charlie."

"How did that go?"

"Not great. Miranda and I were in the group with Charlie and another guy. Let's just say we weren't all on the same page. They were basically treating us like we didn't know what we were talking about."

"That sucks. What were they saying?"

"They were just rushing through the review. Charlie gave me a 'that's so easy' remark when I had a question."

"Oh man, I'm sorry,' he says.

"It's just frustrating."

"Some guys are like that in the office but for the most part the women are well-respected. It won't always be like that."

"I hope not. I try to ignore it."

"That's good," he says, standing up from the kitchen table. "You're awesome and I love you."

I smile at him. "Aww shucks, you're awesome and I love you too."

As I flip through the mail I start to think about Kat. I don't normally relate to kids, probably because I was the youngest and I didn't see my younger cousins growing up. I guess that's why Miranda thinks I don't like them. Kat was really nice though. I suppose if we did have kids I wouldn't mind terribly if we had a girl like her. Spunky and artsy, but sweet and polite. I guess that wouldn't be so terrible.

"Hey babe, I'm gonna go out for a minute. I'll be back soon," I call out to Cullen who's in the bedroom.

"Okay," he calls back.

Stepping outside I see a group of boys practicing their skateboarding tricks in the street. One boy, maybe fifteen or so, is trying to flip his skateboard in a full rotation and have it land on its wheels but isn't having much luck. His friends are riding back and forth trying to hop on the curb and hop off in one graceful maneuver. They don't notice that I'm watching them and seeing them fail repeatedly. It must take hours of practice just to land one small trick. In a way, I admire their determination.

When I get to the house, I see a "Spoiled Dogs Live Here" sign hanging on the door and ivy creeping up the brick facade. Almost as soon as I knock the door swings open.

"Hi, Alice."

"Hey, Melanie."

6

"To the end of finals!" Miranda calls out with a clink of our glasses.

"Hear, hear" I reciprocate.

We chose to celebrate the end of our quarter and our success in passing Mason's class with drinks at *The Grass Skirt*, a dive tiki bar downtown. Jacob recommended it after attending a happy hour here with some coworkers.

"It's awful and wonderful at the same time," he told us. "The waitresses literally wear grass skirts and there are palm trees in every square inch of the place. But the drinks are great. You've gotta get the Devil's Brew because it's amazing. They serve it in a coconut. You can't go there if you're not gonna get a drink in a coconut," he enthusiastically told us on our way out tonight.

"I can't believe we did it, Alice. We have only one quarter left and then it's over. O-ver!"

"I *can* believe it. We studied so much! I don't think I slept at all the week before the final. Cullen is an angel for putting up with me. I was so stressed."

69

Miranda takes a sip of her drink. "Well, we're all done now," she says. "Just a few more classes and we're free from homework and tests and studying. Oh man, remember life without studying? What will I do with my extra time?"

"I guess you can focus on the wedding plans."

"Yeah, something fun for a change," Miranda says, half-joking. "So, tell me about your new tutoring job. You start tomorrow?"

"Yep, Kat. She's in fifth grade. When I met with her mom last week, she was so happy to hear I wanted to help them. Kat is having a hard time right now. She's lost her confidence around math and I guess she used to really like it."

"She's lucky to have you then. I bet you're gonna be great for her. She sounds a lot like you."

"Yeah, I was about her age when I started having a hard time in math. Luckily in high school, I had some great teachers who pushed me. I don't think I'd be where I am today without them."

"You wouldn't be in *The Grass Skirt* without them? That's a shame."

"Haha," I say, dismissing her bad joke. "Well, I wouldn't be here with you, that's for sure."

"Well then, here's to the high school teachers that came before you," she pauses, "and the high school teachers that will come after you."

"That makes absolutely no sense." Our glasses clink again. "Cheers."

Miranda and I reflect over the last few months,

some of it good, some of it not. We're ready to put this last quarter behind us and are hoping for a better experience during our final few months of school. It's so great spending time with Miranda without textbooks and homework that I lose track of the time.

It's nearly eleven o'clock when I tiptoe inside, trying not to wake Cullen. Rick Moranis hops off the coffee table where he likes to stretch out and comes over to rub up against my legs. I drop my keys in the bowl, letting them mingle with spare change and nearly empty Chapstick tubes.

"Hey buddy," I whisper, happy to feel his soft fur and hear his audible purring. "Are you hungry?" I ask, walking into the kitchen. "Me too."

Cullen must have heard the uncontrollable beeping of the microwave as I zapped last night's spaghetti.

"You're home late," Cullen says, squinting his eyes to the kitchen light.

"I know. I'm sorry to wake you," I say whispering, even though he's already awake.

"Did you guys have fun?"

"Mmm-hmm." I'm so tired I can barely answer. "I'm just gonna get something to eat. I'll come to bed soon."

"Okay." He fills a glass with water and returns into the darkness, Rick Moranis following behind.

I probably shouldn't have stayed out so long tonight, but it was great to celebrate with Miranda. She was in rare form. She was so relieved to be done with

Mason's class. Our exam went well, and we were so exhausted but exhilarated when it was all over. We studied until just about the last minute, spending the morning of the exam at our usual place on the bench outside of class. Front row b-, er, Charlie strolled in like it was any other day, which was annoying but oddly reassuring. I suppose if he was as nervous as we were then we'd probably have something to worry about. He'd be our canary in a coal mine, alerting us to danger.

I wasn't thinking about much else last week, except for my upcoming tutoring session with Kat. I can still hear the excitement in Melanie's voice that afternoon when I went over to tell her I was available to help. It was a brief exchange, but Melanie told me that Kat is sometimes bored with her homework, and when things are hard, she tends to give up easily. She gets frustrated sometimes, especially with word problems. I'm excited to work with her, although I'm a little nervous because I've never worked as a tutor before. I wasn't sure what I was getting myself into but the idea of helping a young girl with math seemed rewarding.

Saturday morning I'm up early despite my late night with Miranda. I feel a little anxious about tutoring, but Kat seemed like a cool kid, so it should be an entertaining hour if nothing else. I just hope I can help. I mean, I can do the math on my own, but could I teach someone else?

Before I leave for Kat's house, I grab a blank notepad and some pencils, throw on my yellow

Converse sneakers and a jacket, then head out the door. Shutting the door behind me I can see Daisy outside, but I'm determined to be on time and not get sucked into a conversation that will make me late.

"Miss Alice, good morning! Or is it afternoon?"

"Not yet, just a few minutes before actually." I continue to walk past her hoping to show her that I'm on my way somewhere and can't stop to talk.

"Where are you headed?"

"Oh, well, I'm actually tutoring Kat down the street at noon. I should get going though, I don't want to be late."

"You took the job! Good for you!"

"Thanks, yeah, I finished my finals this week, so I talked to Melanie about helping. It's no big deal."

"Sure it is! Oh, Alice, this is so great."

Daisy had a way of making too big a deal about things. Besides, what if it wasn't great? This could be a disaster.

"Well, I gotta run. See you, Daisy!" I say as I pick up my pace. As I approach Melanie's door, I have a slightly unsettling feeling in my stomach. Shortly after I knock, I hear a shuffle of feet and a muffled voice saying, "It's Alice! She's here!"

The door swings open and Kat is there to greet me and welcome me inside. Her house opens up into a small entryway where there are shoes, big and small, stacked in little cubbies. In their alley kitchen, there's a black refrigerator covered in family photos and drawings from a child's sketchpad.

"Hey, Alice! Guess what?" Kat's eyes are wide, and she has a big smile on her face.

"What?"

"I got a new engineering set last week! Do you wanna see it?"

"Sure, I'd love to."

"Hi Alice," Melanie says, peeking around the corner from the living room. "How about asking our guest if she would like to take her coat off first," she says to Kat. "And see if she'd like something to drink."

"Alice, would you like something to drink?" Kat asks me in a lowered voice.

"No, that's okay, thank you for asking," I tell her, trying to make it sound like it was her idea to ask.

"Are you sure? Water? Tea? I'm happy to make some coffee," Melanie says.

"No, I'm fine, really."

"See, she's fine," says Kat. "C'mon Alice! Let me show you my room." And with that, we're off. She races up the stairs to her bedroom and I try to keep up with her but almost lose her when she turns the corner. Inside her aqua blue painted room, she has art supplies and drawings out on a small white table and bookshelves packed to the top. There are wooden blocks of all shapes and sizes with large plastic nuts and bolts, and ropes and pulleys spread out on the floor.

"This is my new engineering set. Isn't it cool?" she asks, grabbing tools and blocks and showing me all the parts and pieces. "I'm making a Rube Goldberg machine," she tells me, pulling out her drawing plans for the intricate design.

"Wow, this is really impressive. Where did you get the idea to make this?"

"My mom told me about them. In India, they made one of the largest Rube Goldberg machines that took three hundred and one steps to turn on a light! It was so cool!"

I try to match her excitement. "That's awesome. What is yours gonna do?"

"Mine is gonna feed my dog. In the end, this arm is gonna swing around and knock over a cup with his food in it and dump it into his bowl," she says, pointing to her plans.

"Very cool! I can't wait to see this when it's done."

Kat looks up at me. "You could help me with it if you want to."

"Yeah, maybe. It sounds like fun," I tell her. "Well, should we get down to business? Do you have any math homework?"

Reluctantly, Kat puts down her engineering plans and takes a worksheet out of a green backpack on the floor.

"We're doing fractions in school," she tells me. "I don't really get it though."

"Ok, let's take a look." I look at her worksheet that says "Dividing Fractions" at the top. There are ten problems on the page with room to write underneath. Most look identical to one another except for the numbers being different, but they're all set up the same way.

"Alright, well, let's start with number one. Can you show me how you would do this?"

Kat looks at the page for a few seconds trying to remember how to solve the problem. "Our teacher said to do something to one of the numbers, like, you flip it or something? I don't know what she's talking about though."

Deciphering her description of the algorithm, I explain what I assume Kat meant. "Okay, so she probably told you to keep the first fraction the same and then multiply by the reciprocal of the one you're dividing by," I tell her, writing things out on my notepad as I'm telling her.

"Yeah, she used that word! I forgot. I didn't know what it meant."

"Well, it's like reciprocating, which means to give back in return. Like, I give something to you, and then you give something to me." I show her a back and forth motion with my hands, flipping from one hand over the other and then flipping back. "See, it looks a little like flipping the fraction, or taking the *reciprocal*." I emphasize the word so that she understands how to use the proper math terminology.

Kat nods and says, "okay, that makes sense."

"But let's look at it a different way. When I ask you, what is ten divided by five, what would you say is the answer?"

"It's two because five goes into ten two times."

"Exactly, and division works the same way

76

when you work with fractions," I tell her. "So, how many times does one half go into three?"

"Hmm." Kat looks puzzled.

"Start with one. How many times does one half go into one?"

"Twice because two halves make a whole."

"So, how many times does one half go into two?"

She thinks for a moment. "If it goes into one, twice, then it goes into two, four times."

"Great! Now, what about three?"

"That would be six times."

"Perfect! Let's try six divided by one half on your page, but let's use the reciprocal."

Kat follows the steps that her teacher showed her in school, now understanding what to do. "Hey! We got the same answer!" Kat says with surprise.

"Yeah, it works the same way. You can follow the steps, which is called an algorithm, or you can think about the numbers and break it down into the parts. Let's try the next one." I'm pleased to see that Kat is trying to work out the question the same way we did the first one together. After a few problems, she switches to using the steps her teacher showed her.

"This is easy now. I was confused when my teacher was telling us because it didn't make sense."

I begin to wonder if a lot of her assignments look similar to this one. "Do you guys do a lot of worksheets like this?"

"Yes. We used to play games when I was in first

and second grade. Now we mostly do worksheets and it's kind of boring."

"That's too bad," I say. "I study math in college. It's hard but I like it."

Melanie knocks softly on the door and brings in a small yellow plate with grapes and crackers on it.

"Here Kat. Alice, are you sure I can't get you anything?"

"I'm good, thank you," I say. Melanie is hovering a bit and looking at what we're doing. I can tell that she's wondering how our session is going.

"Momma, look, I can divide fractions now!" Kat says, handing her the nearly completed homework assignment.

"Oh honey, this is great! I'm so proud of you, but I knew you could do it. You just need to stick with it."

"Alice showed me how."

Melanie smiles at me. "I knew she could help you," she tells Kat. "Well, keep going, you're doing a great job." She hands her back the worksheet and slips out the door, closing it gently behind her. Kat and I continue until she has all the problems worked out. Before I leave, I review what we've discussed and ask her to come up with a real situation where she would have to divide fractions. It takes her a minute or so to come up with an example, but eventually she tells me about a time when she was baking with her mom and they had to divide the recipe in half. At the time, her mom figured it all out for her but Kat says she could do it on her own now. It's so nice to see how proud of herself she is and I'm happy that I was successful in helping her to understand what was confusing her.

Downstairs I meet with Melanie in the kitchen to let her know we're done and report on what we accomplished. I tell her what a great kid Kat is and how much fun it was to work with her.

"I'm so glad this worked out. She was so excited to see you today. Thank you so much for your help."

"It's my pleasure," I tell her.

"So, if you're interested, we'd love to have you back. Can you work with Kat a few more times, just to get her through the end of the school year?"

"Yeah, I can definitely do that." I think for a moment. "Next Saturday, same time?"

"Sounds good. Thank you so much!"

On the way home I'm practically skipping down the street. This couldn't have gone better. Kat is a sweet kid and we actually hit it off. I don't know why I was so worried.

"Hey, how did it go?" Cullen asks when I get back home.

"It was great actually. We did her homework together. She's working on dividing fractions and I was able to explain it to her." I try to sound humble but I'm pretty proud of myself.

"Honey, that's great news! Oh, I'm so glad."

"Yeah, Melanie wants me to keep working with her. I'm gonna go back next Saturday."

"That's awesome. I'm so proud of you."

"Thanks, yeah, I'm proud of me too," I say with a little laugh. It sounds weird to admit that, but it's true. I mean, I'm not curing cancer here, but I made a difference, even just for a day. Hopefully Kat will go back to school with a better understanding of fractions. "Oh, also, Kat's making a Rube Goldberg machine," I tell him. "She showed me this cool engineering set that she has. It's awesome! It has a ton of differently shaped pieces and it looks like you can make pretty much anything with it."

"Oh right, isn't her mom an engineer?"

"Yeah, I guess she taught her about Rube Goldberg machines. I totally love that. Kat showed me her design plans."

"Wow, that's impressive. When I was young, I had an Erector Set but I would just take out the pieces and start making something. I never really had a plan." He thinks for a moment and I know he's picturing his younger self playing with his toys spread out on the floor. "I miss that set actually. I used to play for hours as a kid."

"I didn't have anything like that when I was young," I tell him. "I only wanted a baby doll and an Easy-Bake Oven."

"Hmm, weird," he says. "You don't like babies or baking."

"I know, right?" I say with a laugh. "It doesn't make any sense."

Part Two

7

"Good morning class. Welcome to Number Theory. My name is Jane Freeman, but you can call me Jane. Please take a copy of the syllabus and pass them down." It's the first day of my new class: five girls and twenty-three guys. Not a huge shift in the balance, but I'll take it. Jane came in all business and owning the room, but it seems like she stepped right off the stage of her high school graduation. I was surprised by how young she looked, especially compared to most of the professors here. She's also the first professor I've seen with tattoos. They were just on her right arm, a flower pattern that went from her shoulder to her elbow with a hummingbird on her bicep. Her long brown hair is casually swooped into a twist and secured on the back of her head with a butterfly-shaped clip. Jane had the confidence and casualness of a veteran teacher but a youthfulness that made her seem approachable.

Miranda and I were excited to be in this class because we heard so many positive things about Jane. Everyone who took her class said that she was firm but fair, easy to understand, and her classes were entertaining and enjoyable. We heard that Jane's classes were in high demand, which was obvious when the class was full and we ended up on the waitlist. I was afraid we weren't going to get in, but we were happy that we both got a spot in the class a few days before the quarter started. Plus, this was our last quarter and we needed the class to graduate, so, needless to say, we were thrilled to be in this class.

As with most classes, Jane begins by reading the syllabus. I'm always a little overwhelmed on the first day of classes. You hear the entire class schedule and all the assignments laid out in front of you on a few sheets of paper. Jane begins, "this course will explore many topics in number theory including elements of numeric and algorithmic work as well as proofs of various sorts. Students will develop skills in conjecture formation, finding counterexamples, and providing proofs using different techniques such as induction, contradiction, proof by cases, and direct implication." She continues, "in addition to the textbook, here are a few books that may be of interest as supplemental or background reading." She gives us a brief list saying that one of the books is "a delightful little book and a fun read." Delightful? Fun? These are not words I hear too often in a math class. I can already tell that this is going to be an interesting course.

Most professors spend the first day reading the syllabus and talking about the plans for the quarter, but Jane jumped right into the first lesson. I like the way she teaches because it feels like she includes the class in the discussion, rather than simply talking to us the whole time. I can already tell by her demeanor that she's going to be more approachable than Mason. Miranda and I always had a hard time asking questions in his class, like we were bothering him or something.

Walking out of class Miranda seems happy, almost excited. "That was a great class!"

"Yeah, it was actually. I really like Jane," I say.

"I like her too," says Miranda. "I'm looking forward to this class. Hopefully, she lives up to the hype."

"I know. So many students have recommended her. We'll see I guess."

Miranda looks at me suddenly as if she just remembered something. "Oh! How was tutoring this weekend?"

"Oh yeah! It was fun. Kat is super cool and I think I was actually able to show her something new, so that felt good. Her mom is super nice. She asked if I would keep working with Kat to get her through the end of the school year. So, I'm gonna go back again on Saturday."

"Alice, that's so great! I'm so glad to hear it worked out." Miranda seems genuinely happy for me.

"Yeah, it wasn't so bad," I tell her.

"You worry too much," Miranda informs me.

"What do you mean?"

"Well, you didn't think you were gonna be a good tutor, but it sounds like you did great. Like how you worried about Mason's tests and you passed no problem."

"I don't know that I passed no problem, but I guess that worked out too."

"You need to start believing in yourself more."

"Yeah, yeah. Okay, Tony Robbins"

"Awaken the giant within!" Miranda says with a commanding tone, quoting the title of one of Tony Robbins's books that her mom used to read.

"Rawgh!" I say, pretending to be a giant.

Since there's a stop on my bus route, I'm able to hit the public library on the way home. I want to take a look at some of the books on Jane's "delightful and fun" reading list. Let's just see how subjective those words can be. I like Jane already, though, so I'm willing to take her word for it and give the books a shot.

I genuinely enjoy being at the library. I'm surrounded by endless amounts of knowledge, stories, and adventures that are waiting around every corner. I get lost in the titles and the smell. Oh, the smell! I love the smell of books. It's the smell of old pages that have been read by so many before me. Plus, nothing beats the softness of a worn-out book. A brand-new book seems sad like no one has taken it for a test drive yet. But, a broken-in book is a vintage car with character.

In the Academics section I find one of the books on Jane's list and flipping through it I decide to give it a try. Looking for the second book something grabs my attention. It's an orange book with "What's Math Got To Do With It" written down the spine and "math" outlined in dots like a flashing neon sign. The subtitle grabs me the most, "How Parents and Teachers Can Help Children Learn to Love Their Least Favorite Subject". The author, Jo Boaler, has a pretty impressive bio on the inside cover, and the more I look through the contents the more interested I am. There's a chapter about better classroom strategies and activities in the back of the book. Whoa, a chapter about girls in math and science! I don't hear a lot of people talking about women in math. This should be interesting. I definitely have to check this out.

This book gets me thinking about math being students' least favorite subject'. Why is that? Why did I love math as a kid when others hated it? What made me dislike it the way so many others did when I got to middle school? Oddly, I never thought about it too much. I rekindled my love of math and that was all that mattered. It wasn't until high school that I started to like it again, but I never thought I would major in math. It didn't seem like a path I wanted to choose. Even when I told friends that I was starting college and wanted to study math, so many were shocked, even though I did well in high school. I thought I might be an artist or a writer. I pictured myself as a free-spirit, a creative type who wasn't tied down by anything and would wander the country looking for inspiration. It's funny how things change.

Although the remaining bus ride home is only a few minutes, I'm already deep into the first chapter by the time I reach my final stop. Once I get inside the house, I say hello to Rick Moranis before pouring myself a cup of this morning's coffee and zap it in the microwave. Settling in on the couch I'm right back into the book again where I left off. It's fascinating already. In the first chapter, Jo talks about a math teacher, Emily, who was giving her student's a better way to learn math. The students were working out problems by asking questions and being engaged. This doesn't sound like a typical classroom. The chapter ends by saying that despite Emily's awards for teaching, her school no longer allowed her to teach in this way. Man, what a huge loss for those students. I haven't had many experiences like the one described in this book, except for Mrs. Hayes, my elementary school science teacher. I get to thinking about how amazing her class was and wonder how she's doing.

"Maybe I should write to her, or find out where she lives and stop by," I think. That might be a little strange though, I haven't seen her in years. I doubt she'd even remember me. Plus, she's been sick, and I wouldn't want to bother her. A letter though, that might be nice. Hopefully, she'll appreciate that. I wonder how many teachers actually get thanked for their work and for inspiring their students. Sadly, it's probably a small number.

It's hard to get started writing a letter to someone I haven't seen in over fifteen years, but once I start writing I can't stop. All sorts of memories come flooding back and I tell her how much fun her class was and how I never forgot the experience. I haven't had that much fun in school since then and I want to tell her how much

I admire her. I'm not sure where to send the letter though. I started writing before I was able to find her address.

I look online to see if there's a listing in the Portland area, but I get too many results. I have no idea which listing is hers and it's possible none of them are the correct address. Come to think of it, maybe Mr. Grant knows where she lives. He knew she was sick after all. When I finish writing my letter to Mrs. Hayes I decide to run down to the market and see if Mr. Grant can help me.

"Alice, how are you?" asks Mr. Grant.

"I'm good, thanks. I was wondering if you happen to know where Mrs. Hayes lives?"

"Mrs. Hayes?"

"Yeah, the science teacher, er, well, she was the science teacher. Remember, you told me she was sick last month?"

"Yes, of course. Why do you want to know where she lives?"

"Well, I got to thinking about her and I wrote her a letter to thank her for a wonderful class. She was a great teacher and I want her to know how much I appreciate her and the way she taught us. It's kind of weird, I dunno. She probably doesn't even remember me."

"No, that's sweet. Of course she remembers you!" he says. "I don't know where she lives, but her granddaughter, Erin, comes in here about once a week. If you want, you can leave the letter here and I'll give it to her for you."

"Oh yes! That would be wonderful, thank you so much." After I hand Mr. Grant the letter, I grab my usual *Loafing Around* sandwich before heading back to the house. I start to feel a little silly about writing Mrs. Hayes a letter after all this time, but I hope she's doing okay. Hopefully, she'll appreciate a kind word from one of her former students. Actually, I hope it takes her a long time to even get to my letter because there are so many letters for her to sift through, like fan letters for a movie star. Maybe there are crates of letters coming in every day and she says, "Oh Erin! My students are so kind as to write to me. How wonderful it is to be so beloved!" It's a ridiculous thought but it pleases me to think about Mrs. Hayes, the back of her hand over her forehead, about to collapse from the overwhelming joy of it all.

I smile at the thought of old Mrs. Hayes with stacks of letters at her feet, piled so high she can barely open the front door anymore. Perhaps I will have fan letters waiting for me when I get home. Wouldn't that be a thrill! Lifting the metal lid to the mailbox I see that, in fact, no one has sent me a letter at all. Nothing but ads and junk mail, except there's an envelope for Cullen, the address written by hand.

Rather than reading an exciting fan letter, I take out my notes from our first class with Jane and study for a bit. It's only been one class, but I want to make sure I'm staying ahead. I only have a few classes left to graduate and it's important that I do well. Looking over the syllabus one more time I see that our first assignment is due next week. Maybe Miranda and I can work together on it. It's gonna be so weird not having her to rely on next year. Hopefully, we'll both be working at amazing jobs. It would be even more amazing if we ended up in the same place so we could commute to work together and gossip around the water cooler. I don't know if offices still have water coolers, but I'm going to imagine it anyway.

"Hey, you're home early," I say to Cullen as he walks in the door.

"Yeah, we finished early today. I decided to make it a half-day since I worked overtime last week."

"Well, it's nice to have you home," I say with a smile. "There's a letter for you on the table."

Cullen picks up the envelope, opens it, and pulls out a postcard-sized photo that has writing on the back. There was no return address, so I don't know who the sender is.

"Who's it from?" I ask.

There's a long pause before he tells me, "Kristen. She's coming to visit."

"Your sister's coming? When?" I ask Cullen.

"At the end of June."

"Wow, that's great news! We haven't seen her since we went to Palo Alto last year."

"She says there's a conference in Portland that she's coming to," he says. "She wants to know if she can stay with us."

"Absolutely!" I say without hesitation.

"Are you sure? You know she can be a handful," he says. It's true that Kristen is a ball of energy, but that's what I like most about her. She's impulsive and quirky, not at all like Cullen who's the sensible one of the family, but she's so much fun to be around.

"She's not a handful, babe. She's...spirited."

"To say the least. I guess I'll give her a call and tell her she can stay with us if you're sure."

"Of course I'm sure. Call her. Now!"

8

"You have to meet Kristen, she's awesome," I say to Miranda after class. We're meeting to go over the first assignment. Jane assigned it today and we want to get a head start, even though it's not due for a week.

"More awesome than I am?" she asks.

"Not more, exactly. Just, a different kind of awesome."

"Nice save, Gretzky."

"But seriously, you're gonna love her."

"Is Cullen excited to see her?"

"I guess." I don't sound too convincing. "I dunno, they don't have a lot in common."

"Well, it's cool that she's coming. Will she be here for graduation?" Miranda asks.

"No, I think she's coming the week after."

"Bummer."

"Yeah, but that's okay. I'm still excited she's coming," I say.

Kristen is a few years older than Cullen and I

always love seeing her. Last year we stayed with her and her husband, Brandon, at their new house in Palo Alto. She had just finished getting her Master's in Education and they moved into this great little neighborhood right before we saw them. I can't wait to see her again. Plus, I'll be done with school by the time she gets here so we can hit the town and I won't have to worry about my classwork.

The last time I saw her we stayed up until almost two o'clock in the morning talking and laughing. I was telling her about school, and she was asking me about my plans, or actually my lack of plans. I guess that hasn't changed much for me because I still don't know what I want to do. It's like that man on the bus last month. I tell everyone that there's so much I can do with a math degree, but honestly, it's a little scary. I don't feel like I have a clear destination. A mathematician? I barely know what that means. I don't know where I'll work or what exactly I'll be doing. I've been so stressed with classes this last year that I haven't been able to think about what I'm gonna do next.

"So, what do you think of Jane so far?" Miranda asks.

"I like her. I surprisingly understand what she's talking about. She does a great job of explaining things."

"Yeah, I agree."

"Oh! And today, remember when she asked, 'isn't this fun?' when she was talking about conjecture? I actually thought it *was* fun! I looked around the room because I thought others would agree, but the look on most people's faces was confusion. No one else seemed to think it was fun."

"Oh yeah, I laughed when she said that. I actually didn't think it was all that fun," Miranda says, holding up her hands to make air quotes.

"Really? I did. I'm already loving this class."

Miranda laughs. "It's only our second class, how do you love it already?"

"I don't know. I just do."

Being in Jane's class has been great. She has this incredible energy and I feel like we have a lot in common. I can relate to her. Actually, in class today she saw Jo Boaler's book on my desk, and we started talking about it.

"That's a great book," Jane said.

"Yeah, I know. I mean, I just started the other day but I really like it. I can't put it down."

"I read it when I was an undergrad too," she tells me. "Well, enjoy it. Let me know what you think when you're done."

This might have been one of the first real conversations I've had with any of my teachers so far. Of course, I've talked to instructors about the course or an assignment or a grade, but that's about it. It's cool to have a teacher I can converse with. Jane seems like someone Miranda and I would have a drink with. Maybe she's a regular at *The Grass Skirt*!

"What do you guys have planned for this weekend?" Miranda asks looking up from her notebook.

"Not a whole lot. I have my tutoring session

with Kat on Saturday and then on Sunday I usually get the house to myself when Cullen goes to band practice. I'll probably just be on the couch with Rick Moranis.

Miranda laughs. "Man, his career has really taken a dive."

"Oh, so hilarious." Miranda is not tired of making some version of this joke.

"Ok, I'll stop joking that the actor is living in your house," she says, sad that her oh-so-funny comedy career is coming to an end. "How's it going with Kat?"

"Great actually. We've met twice now. She's cool. Oh hey, did I tell you she's making a Rube Goldberg machine?"

"A what?"

"You know, those chain reaction machines. Like, you drop a ball, it hits a thing, then rolls down and knocks something over, and at the end it completes a goal of some kind," I tell her, acting out the motions with my hands.

"Um, yeah, I think I know what you mean."

"Well, Kat is making one that feeds her dog."

"That's incredible! I wanna see that."

"Yeah, it sounds awesome. She told me I could help her make it," I inform her.

"Oh wow, let me know how it goes."

I was thinking about Kat this week and started to brainstorm some ideas for her machine. Last Saturday she had already started construction but was having some trouble getting a marble to slide into the little stacked blocks she wanted to knock over. She was doing a lot of problem-solving and trying to come up with new ideas, making modifications to her plan.

When I arrived at Kat's last Saturday, she was excited to see me and I had to admit, I was excited to see her too. We're making a lot of progress with fractions and not only is she doing well, but I feel like I'm accomplishing something by working with her. It feels good to help her with math, but I also genuinely enjoy spending time with her.

"Hi, c'mon in. You must be Alice." I was greeted at Kat's door by a new face, a tall man, slender, man wearing a navy cardigan and faded blue jeans. "I'm Kat's dad, Luke."

"Oh hi, I've heard a lot about you. We finally meet." It had been almost two months since they moved in down the street and even though I had been to the house a few times, Luke and I had never crossed paths.

"I've heard a lot about you too," he says. "It sounds like Kat is enjoying working with you."

"Oh, thanks, that's so nice to hear," I say. "It's been fun so far."

"Well, Kat is in her room if you'd like to go up," he tells me, but before I can respond, Kat barrels down the stairs making rhythmic thuds as she hits each step.

"Alice! I did it! Come look," she says, nearly out of breath.

"What's going on?" I ask.

"My Rube Goldberg machine! I got the blocks to knock over. I made a track for the marble and I had to test it a few times because it wouldn't line up, but I got it! Come check it out!" She's excited and talking so fast that I can barely follow what she's saying.

"Okay, let's go look," I say. I turn back to Luke. "It was nice meeting you. I guess I'll see you later," and with that Kat leads me upstairs and shows me the new contraption she's been working on.

"See, watch," she says and lets the marble drop into the first tube, letting gravity pull it down and it slides across the track, hits the blocks exactly, and rolls to the next destination.

"This is so great!" I'm impressed with how well she set this up. "How long did this take you to work out?"

"About two days. I had to make the track out of these wood pieces but it wasn't the right length, so I had to move all the blocks and I kept knocking them down and setting them up again. I had to test it so many times, but I finally got it to work."

"Kat, this is really impressive. I'm so glad you stuck with it and kept trying. See what happens when you don't give up?"

"I know. It was hard to get it figured out though."

"Well, I'm happy to see what you came up with," I tell her, setting down my backpack and getting out my notebook and pencil. "Okay, so let's get started on your math homework. What are you working on right now?"

"I have this worksheet," she tells me, grabbing a

piece of paper off of her desk. A few of the problems were worked out but Kat tells me she got bored and gave up.

"Let's look," I say. Reviewing the first few problems, I can see she made a few mistakes.

"Can you tell me how you got this answer?" I ask, pointing to one of the problems.

"Ok," she says. "So, first you have to see how many times four goes into five. Then you write the four here and subtract. Then you bring down the eight," she says, drawing an arrow down. "Then...wait." She thinks for a minute and tries to retrace her steps. "I don't actually remember what I did next."

Knowing the proper steps for long division I can make sense of her work and see where she left off. "Ok, so I see you have a four on the top here. Do you know where that came from?" I ask, seeing if she can start back at the beginning.

"Oh, um, I think that came from the eighteen?" She thinks for a few seconds. "Oh yeah, four goes into eighteen four times, so you put the four up here." Kat points to the four she wrote on top of the long division symbol. "After that, I'm kind of confused.

"So, you said you got bored. Were you maybe simply confused and that's why you stopped?" I ask, trying to be sensitive.

Kat pauses for a moment. "Kind of. It doesn't make sense."

"Okay, so let's look at this a different way." I work with Kat for a few minutes, giving her a new way to look at division. Instead of going through the steps that she was taught, I have her look at the numbers she's dividing and ask her how many groups of four fit inside. She counts more and more fours, adding them all up, then when she reaches her goal, she's able to find an answer.

Questioning this new strategy, she asks, "so wait, can I always do this?"

"Sure. It might take a little longer, but if it makes sense then try it this way. Let's do the next one together." After twenty minutes she's got it down and is working independently on her homework but still verifying her answers with me. I can see, however, that she's trying to rush towards the end of the worksheet and starts to make a few errors. "Take your time though. You don't have to rush, or you'll make mistakes."

"Okay," she says.

I'm really pleased with how well she's working and by the time she's on the last problem our hour is up.

"That's the end of our time Kat. How are you feeling about the work you did?"

"Good. I understand now."

I'm glad she's able to complete her homework, but it's a bit depressing watching her do a worksheet every time. She was so excited talking about her Rube Goldberg machine, but the minute we started her homework her whole attitude changed. It's no wonder that she's bored with math and she must be a lot less motivated when she's confused. I'm glad I can be here for Kat. It makes me think about Miranda and how we've been able to support each other.

"Well, thanks for working so hard today, Kat," I say as I'm gathering my things to leave. "Good luck on your Rube Goldberg machine."

"Can you come back tomorrow to work on it with me?" Kat asks.

"Sure. Let me check with your dad, okay?"

"Okay."

"See you later, Kat."

"Bye Alice, thank you."

9

"You'll be getting back your midterms today," Jane informs the class. "Overall, the grades were pretty good. If you didn't pass, you'll see a note on your test asking for a meeting with me during office hours. I expect to see any of you that need the extra help."

Miranda and I look at each other feeling confident that we weren't going to be students with notes on our tests. We had been studying like crazy and after class last week we walked out with our heads held high, feeling confident that we did well.

"Nice work," says Jane as she hands me my test.

Miranda turns to me. "We did it!" she tells me and shows me her grade.

"Yes! Congrats." I'm happy that Miranda and I get to rejoice together. This feels so much better than Mason's midterm when Miranda failed. I like when we succeed together.

I'm really enjoying this class so far. I can tell that Jane is passionate about what she's teaching, and she explains things in a real context. I feel connected to the material. Normally I just follow along and try to grasp the ideas, but now I feel that I fully understood what I'm learning. I hope this feeling continues.

After class, I see a flyer on the job postings bulletin board that catches my eye. Looking it over, it seems too good to be true. There's a company in Seattle that offers creative math camps for girls and they're looking for summer instructors.

"Miranda, look at this," I say, pointing to the flyer.

"Wow. A math program for girls? That's incredible!"

"I keep saying I don't want to teach, but man, that's really cool." I read the rest of the details. "Could you imagine spending the summer trying to show girls how much fun math can be?"

"It sounds awesome," Miranda says. "Are you gonna apply?"

"I dunno, maybe. It says you can run camps locally. I could look into it." I grab the flyer and stuff it into my bag.

Over dinner, I tell Cullen about my grade on the test and the unexpected job possibility. He perks up when I tell him about the position because he knows this could be a good fit for me.

"You should definitely apply," he says.

"Yeah, I'm thinking about it."

He doesn't look convinced. "You don't have anything lined up yet after graduation."

"I know, but I need to start applying for full-time jobs. This is only for a few weeks during the summer."

"But it sounds like a good opportunity," he says. "You could try this and see what happens. Maybe it leads to something more."

"I guess you're right."

He was right, too. I should consider all possibilities, especially since I don't have anything else planned. A summer job was certainly better than nothing. Plus, it did sound like a cool program. After dinner, I check out the company website and I'm blown away. Their whole goal is to get more girls interested in math. That's very dear to my heart, but since I don't want to teach and I don't have experience running camps like this, it's pretty intimidating. Spending the summer with kids doesn't sound like my cup of tea either. Working with Kat is one thing, but I'm not sure that I could handle a group of girls.

"Hey hon, Daisy is here," Cullen calls unexpectedly from the front door. I tear myself away from the computer, a little surprised she's here in the evening. I don't usually see her after dinner.

I peek my head outside where Daisy is standing on the front porch. "Hey, Daisy, what's up?"

"Hi, Alice! I stopped by because I'm heading over to Susan's house. She's having a little ladies' night gathering and I thought you might like to come."

"Oh, um..." I look to Cullen who shrugs, telling me "why not?" with the look on his face. "Sure, I can go for a bit," I tell her.

"Oh, wonderful!" Daisy is thrilled to have me

joining her for once because I almost always say no when she invites me to neighborhood events.

"Let me grab a sweater. I'll be right out."

I was hesitant to come along because I don't know Susan that well. I met her last year at a community garage sale on our block. She seemed nice, but I only met her one time. Apparently, she and Daisy do a lot of community events together.

"Susan is trying to cheer up her sister. She just got divorced so she organized this ladies' night, totally last minute. We all wanted to get together and show our support," Daisy informs me. She tends to do this a lot. A "ladies' night" turns into a gathering of support for someone's divorced sister only after I agree to go. Once she invited me to a "dinner party" that ended up being a BYOB potluck. Sometimes the details are missing in the invitation.

"Sounds like fun, I mean, that's nice of the ladies to support her. I mean, ladies helping ladies, am I right?" I have no idea what to say.

"Absolutely!"

It's a short walk to Susan's house, but on the way, Daisy points out three neighbor's houses and has a story of something that happened to each of them in the last twenty-four hours. I don't know how she does it. I swear, she must subscribe to some sort of newsletter or something. Susan's house is an old cottage-style home with cedar siding and wooden chimes on the front porch that I assume are meant to sound like rain falling. I never understood why people would choose to hang something that makes the same sound we hear six months out of the year naturally. Daisy walks right in the front door without knocking and Susan is in the front room to greet us.

"Daisy! You came!" she says, reaching out her arms to hug Daisy as if she hasn't seen her in a lifetime.

"Susan, you've met Alice before, right?" Daisy asks, motioning me closer.

"Hi, Susan," I say, reaching out to shake her hand. I never know how to greet people and I sometimes think a handshake is too formal, but I can't help myself in an awkward situation.

"Hello, Alice. Yes, I think we met last year at the garage sale. You bought my workout tapes."

"Oh wow, you have a good memory," I say.

"Well ladies, come on in. Grab a drink. We're just getting started." Susan points towards the back of the house. "There are a few others out on the patio if you want to join them."

"Sounds good. Alice, should we head back there?" Daisy asks, pouring herself a glass of wine. "Red or white?"

"White."

On the patio, there are plants everywhere in pots of all shapes and colors. I can see two women talking near a collection of ceramic gnomes in the garden and an older woman sitting on one of the white folding chairs scattered around the patio. She's talking to someone I actually know.

"Melanie, hi! I wasn't expecting to see you."

"Alice, oh my goodness. I wasn't expecting to see you either," she says.

"Yeah, this isn't really my scene, but I thought I'd come," I say, but fear I might have offended her. "I mean, Daisy invited me. I'm happy to be here."

"That's cool. I know what you mean. I'm not big on neighborhood things but since I'm still kind of new in town I thought I'd come by and meet everyone."

"How do you know Susan?" I ask.

"I actually know Susan's sister. Her daughter is in the same class as Kat and I see them at pickup sometimes."

"Oh cool. How's Kat doing?"

"Great. She's adjusting to the new school and she's been doing so much better with her homework, especially in math. I have to give you credit for that."

"Oh no, please. It's all her." I wave my hand to shake away her comment.

"You're too modest."

Daisy sees me talking to Melanie and comes over to say hello. "Melanie, it's nice to see you here tonight."

"You too Daisy. How are you?"

"Can't complain, I suppose."

"Alice and I were just talking about her work with Kat," Melanie informs her. "We're so glad you recommended her to us." I can feel the redness appear on my cheeks. I get uncomfortable when people say nice things about me, especially when I'm right there listening. Also, Daisy is bound to give me an I-told-you-so look as she takes credit for recommending me.

"Oh, I knew she would be a great tutor! Alice, you're doing a great thing. Girls need a role model like you," Daisy says.

"I don't think I'm a role model exactly."

"Nonsense. You're a young girl studying math. It's so impressive." I don't quite know how I feel about this. It sounds like a compliment, but it comes out like an insult. Is she impressed by my ability to do math or the fact that I'm a girl in the math program?

"Well, thanks. I like working with Kat," I tell them.

"She loves working with you too," says Melanie.

Susan comes out to join us on the patio and I'm glad the focus has shifted off of me. Her sister walks out behind her and there's a striking resemblance. Looking around at the group, I don't feel like I really fit in here. I'm the youngest by far and this isn't my usual type of gathering. Being social isn't my strong suit and the fake smile I have on most of the night is getting exhausting. I'm glad Melanie is here but other than chatting with her, I don't have much to contribute to the conversation.

We spend most of the evening outside where the other women mingle and share their condolences with Susan's sister over her divorce. It turns out her daughter, Holly, is a playdate regular with some of the women who have also have daughters around her age. I can only take the small talk for so long when I decide to use the excuse of an early morning class to head home early.

Later that night I can't help but think about what

Daisy said. I don't want to stand out as a girl who likes math. I wish it was a normal thing, but I guess I do stand out. When I do a head count of the girls in class on the first day, we're always the minority. Even Jane is one of the few female math teachers I've had. I guess that's part of why I like her so much.

Thinking more about that summer job I decide it's too good to pass up. Even if it doesn't lead to anything, I think it would be a rewarding experience. Besides, it will give me some extra money this summer which I desperately need.

"Hey hon," I say to Cullen, nearly passing out on the couch when I get home. I'm tired from socializing and the two glasses of wine.

"Hey, how was it?"

"Not bad. I saw Melanie there."

"Oh, that's good."

"Yeah, and actually more than that, I have some news."

10

"So, I contacted the owner of that company that runs the math camps. You know, the summer job?" I tell Miranda before class.

"That's great! Did you find out more about it?"

"Yeah, she emailed me back and wants to discuss the whole thing with me tomorrow. She wants me to call her when I'm free."

"Awesome! Let me know how it goes."

When I got the email from Emma, the owner of the Seattle company, I have to admit I was pretty excited. They're looking to get new people to run the camps and she said she'd give me the curriculum and help me get it started. This was becoming a real possibility.

"Good morning everyone," Jane says. "Today you're gonna work in groups to practice proofs by induction." She walks around the room passing out playing cards, every student getting one card. "If you have an ace card please come to this side of the room," she says, motioning to the front corner. "If you have a two please come to this side of the room. If you have a three, I'd like you back there, and if you have a four please gather over here."

Students begin to collect their belongings and move to their respective corners of the classroom. In my group, the aces, there are four of us, two girls and two guys. The other girl has been quiet throughout the quarter, but I've seen her talking and goofing around with some friends in the hallway before class. One guy is very tall and thin with long hair pulled tight into a bun. This was the first time we were put into groups and sadly the first time any of us had talked to each other.

"Please introduce yourself to your group members and tell them a little about yourself," Jane instructs.

After a few moments of awkward silence, the other girl in my group speaks up. "Hey, um, I guess I'll go first. My name is Sarah and I'm majoring in math education."

"Hi. Chris," says the tall guy. "I'm an engineering major. I just transferred here last winter."

"Alice, math major," I say. "I'm not sure what else, um, I also work as a math tutor." I try to add something interesting but fall short of any original thought.

Last to speak is an older guy, probably in his 30s. He speaks softly and simply says, "Adam." Nothing more.

"Alright, now that you've gotten to know your group, take a look at the screen and begin working on this proof. Before you start talking with your group, take five minutes of private-think-time." She says 'private-think-time' in such an official way, as if this is a standard method of solving a problem. I look at the screen where Jane has projected the theorem we're supposed to prove and begin to write down some ideas. My group members are also writing, some more furiously than others. Sarah isn't writing much, and her eyes are darting around a lot, looking to see what others are writing. After five minutes exactly, Jane asks us to share our ideas with the group.

We all look to each other, but no one wants to speak first. There's a lot of hesitation and uncomfortable smiling.

"Well, I guess I'll go," I say. "Here's what I have so far." I put my paper in the middle of the group and line by line explain what I had been working on. It's uncomfortable being the first person to speak, but I volunteer just to get the ball rolling.

"I think that works, but I was trying to start with the null case," Chris says.

"Oh, you're right. I missed that," I say. I look back at my work and write out the missing information. "Okay, yeah, that works for the null case. What do you guys think?"

I look at the other group members, but Sarah and Adam are very quiet. After a minute or two of reviewing our work, both say that they agree with the way Chris and I are approaching the proof. We're off to a slow start but eventually we piece together what we need and all agree on the final solution.

Each group in class is talking and sharing and there's great energy in the room. We don't usually have math classes like this. I'm usually taking notes the whole time and listening to what the professor is saying. Jane's way of teaching is more casual, but overall, we spend most of the time listening to her lecture. Group work is a bit scary, but it's a nice change of pace.

"I'm gonna start passing around a large piece of paper and some markers to each group," Jane says. "You'll need to write down your proof and then nominate someone to be the presenter."

Markers and paper? I don't think I've used markers since the third grade.

Jane brings our supplies over and again we look at each other in the group, not sure who is going to take the initiative to start writing. Sarah hesitates for a moment but finally volunteers so I give her my paper so she can copy it. We spend a few minutes going through our proof again to make sure Sarah has written everything correctly before we decide who is going to present. Sarah made a smart choice to write everything down. She's off the hook now because she participated, which I can tell she's thinking too because she nudges the paper to the rest of us.

"Adam, do you wanna go up?" I ask. I figure since he was the least involved in the group this would be a good way for him to participate. Of course, I personally don't have any plans to volunteer.

I can tell he doesn't want to go up by the look on

his face, but he finally gives in. "Um, I guess so," he says.

That's a relief! I have a hard time speaking in public and I really don't want to stand in front of the whole class. Even though we worked as a group and agreed on the solution, I don't want to be our representative.

One by one, each group sends up a group member to make their presentation. It's so hard to watch people who are nervous, but without a doubt, I would not want to be in their shoes. Finally, it's Adam's turn. When he gets up there, he doesn't quite know what to say and he's talking so quietly that we can barely hear him. He looks like a deer in headlights and it's a little hard to watch. By the way he's presenting he makes it seem like our group doesn't exactly know what we're talking about. I don't know what force is pulling me up there, but I feel so bad for him that I stand up and walk to the front of the class to rescue him. He's like a comic at an open-mic night and he's bombing! I stumble through the rest of the proof and try not to look out at the class. Jane makes it look so easy to be up here! I can't imagine being in front of the class every day. I catch Miranda's eye and she's giving me a huge, proud smile which helps to calm my nerves. I'm probably only up there for thirty seconds but it feels like an eternity. I can't get back to my seat fast enough when I'm done.

Back at my desk, my group members are all smiling at me. "Good job," says Sarah. There's one more group to go up but I can't focus on what their presenter is saying. All I can think about is the adrenaline rushing through me and how hard it is to talk in front of the class. When the last group is finished, Jane reviews the proof and I'm proud to say that my group members and I nailed it. I guess I didn't look too foolish up there. Jane outlines our next homework assignment before dismissing us, and as I'm collecting my backpack and jacket from the back of my chair, Miranda rushes over to meet me.

"I can't believe you went up there! Nice job!" she says sincerely.

"Oh man, that was so scary. He was dying, I had to save him."

"Well, I was really impressed. You didn't seem nervous at all."

"Are you kidding? I hate public speaking."

"No, you did great."

We walk out together and make our usual stop at the coffee cart. Despite my thirty seconds at the front of the class, I surprisingly had a great time. Working in groups isn't always that fun, but it was cool seeing how everyone did their proof. Jane wasn't teaching us today. She was letting us figure things out for ourselves and it was totally refreshing.

11

My weeks are going by so quickly. I can't believe I already have my sixth session with Kat this afternoon, although it's my seventh time meeting with her. We worked together on her Rube Goldberg machine a few weeks ago. She has the most creative energy. It was great to see the way she was problem-solving and making modifications to her plan when something didn't quite work out. It was so much fun bouncing ideas off of her and seeing what she came up with. Each time I see her is so much fun, but it's more fun just to hang out with this creative personality than it is watching her struggle with math. I know she's not enjoying it. She's stuck in the rules that she learns in school but once we get talking about different methods it's rewarding to see how she changes her mindset. I'm happy to see that she has a much better relationship with math now that she's learning the versatile ways, she can solve a problem.

I have a few hours before I need to be at Kat's house. Cullen and I are stopping by the farmer's market this morning so we're up early for a change. It's a crisp spring day and it's nice to see so many dogs out, released from the confines of their raincoats and little dog sweaters. Even I was freed from my rain gear and we walked down to the market in light layers.

"Oh hey, that's Susan over there, from the ladies' night," I tell Cullen, discreetly pointing to the woman standing by the table of all-natural soaps.

"Do you wanna say hi?" he asks.

"No that's okay. Oh, wait, too late. She saw me." I give Susan a wave and Cullen and I walk towards her. She has canvas tote bags filled to the brim with colorful vegetables that are practically spilling out of the top.

"Hi Susan, how are you?" I ask.

"Alice! Hi, it's nice to see you," she says. "I'm good, how are you doing?"

"Good." I look to Cullen who is shifting his weight from side to side and looking around at the nearby tables. "Susan, this is my boyfriend, Cullen."

"Hi there!" She sticks out her hand, balancing bags across her forearms.

Cullen turns to her and shakes her hand. "Hi, nice to meet you."

"So, Alice, I hear you're tutoring, is that right?" she asks.

"Yes, Kat, she's Melanie's daughter. Actually, I'm going to see her this afternoon."

"Well, are you looking for more work? My niece, Holly, needs help. I think the girls are in class together."

"Oh, yeah, Melanie mentioned her. I wasn't

looking, but I might be able to help," I say, not ready to commit. "I mean, I'm still in school so I don't have a lot of extra time."

"Well, keep me posted. Daisy has my number. If you get some time, I'm sure she'd love to work with you."

"Sure, I'll let you know." I hadn't thought about tutoring as a real job. It only started because Daisy recommended me and things are going so well with Kat that I kept meeting with her.

As we make it to the apple stand Cullen says, "you're really in demand!"

"What? Oh, with tutoring? Yeah, I didn't expect this to turn into anything more than helping Kat for the school year."

"It sounds like you could help other girls too."

"That's true, I guess. I don't know if this is something I want to do in the long run, though. Maybe I'll think about it."

Even though I told him I would think about it, tutoring is basically teaching, which I didn't want to do. Actually, it wasn't even teaching, I was mostly just helping Kat with her homework.

Working with Kat was great, but I had to admit that her homework was a little boring. I could see why she was having a hard time this year. I don't think she was learning in a way that was interesting to her. She was losing focus in class and was missing a lot of the instruction. Each time she pulled a worksheet out of her bag I was uninspired. I could explain the work to her, but the endless practice problems were so mundane. I mean, I love math, but I don't love doing homework. I was almost done with school and ready to be rid of homework assignments. This may not be the best option for me.

After the farmer's market I have a little time to kill and end up looking at the math camp website. I called Emma last week and I was so inspired by the work she's doing. I'm in the process of setting up summer camps with her company and I'm looking forward to seeing their curriculum. I doubt I've seen anything like it before. I finished Jo Boaler's book and it was incredible. I was thinking of trying out some of the activities with Kat.

When I get to Kat's house she's drawing at the desk in her bedroom. From the look of it, she is drafting another project to create with her engineering set. As soon as she sees me she wants to show me her design.

"Hi, Alice! Look what I'm making," she says, handing me her drawing. Looking at the intricate details, it looks like a small vehicle with a propeller on the back and she's included a supply list on the side of the page.

"This looks interesting. Is it a propeller car?" I ask.

"Yes, I want to test different designs to see which one can go the fastest. My friend Justin made one but mine is a three-wheeled car instead of four."

"Well, you definitely have a mind for engineering. I like your design so far." I hand Kat her drawing and get out my supplies for tutoring. "What do you have to work on today? Any math homework?"

Kat doesn't look up from her desk. "No, I had some earlier this week, but I finished it already."

"Oh, okay. Is there anything you feel like we should review?"

"Nope." Hmm, this was unlike her to not have any homework. I'm happy she was able to get her work done on her own, but now I need to figure out a way to make this session productive. Looking around her room I come up with an idea.

"So, Kat, you worked so hard on your Rube Goldberg machine. Do you like doing puzzles?" I ask.

"I love puzzles! Momma and I are always doing jigsaw puzzles together, and I like taking things apart and trying to put them back together."

"That's very cool. I notice you have a chess set over there," I say, pointing to the red box on her bookshelf.

"My dad taught me how to play."

"Well, I have an idea. It's actually a math puzzle. Do you want to try it?" There was an interesting chessboard puzzle in the back of Jo Boaler's book that I wanted to try. I was a little stumped when I tried it myself, so I wanted to see how Kat did with it.

"Sure." Kat grabs the box from the shelf, opens the lid, and starts to remove the plastic game pieces.

"Okay, so we just need the board. Can you tell me how many squares are on here?"

"That's easy, sixty-four." It was an eight-by-eight black and white grid, so naturally, she counted those squares and very quickly gave me her answer.

"Look closer at the board. Do you see any more?" She furrows her brow and gives me a look like I'm a little crazy. "Let's go back a bit. What makes a square a square?"

"It's a shape with four sides."

"Okay, good. And what can you tell me about each side?"

"All the sides are the same length."

"Right. Now, these are the squares you saw, right?" I ask, tracing the small black and white squares with my finger. "There are eight squares across and eight going down."

"Yep, that's how I got sixty-four. If you multiply eight by eight, that's sixty-four." She is very pleased with herself and sounds confident that she got them all.

"You're correct about that. So, this board is an eight-by-eight chessboard. These individual squares are then one-by-one. Do you agree?"

"Yes," she says.

"Then, are there two-by-two squares?"

She looks at the board in a different way and discovers what she had missed the first time. "Yeah! Look, right here," she says, tracing the two-by-two squares with her finger.

"And how many of those do you see?" We work together and I help her find all of the two-by-two squares.

"Great, so now how many three-by-three squares are there?" Around and around we go, working to find all the squares and coming up with a system for finding them all. When we're done, I ask her to look at the pattern. "I've written down the total for all the different sized squares. Can you tell me what you see?"

After a few minutes, Kat's face lights up and her eyes get big. "Oh! There is one eight-by-eight, four seven-by-sevens, nine six-by-sixes and if you keep going you get sixty-four one-by-ones! It's one, four, nine, sixteen, all the way to sixty-four. Those are all perfect squares!"

"Yes, exactly! This is a game of squares! Get it?"

"I get it! That's really cool. Can we go show my mom?"

"Absolutely. Let's go show her." We grab the board and head downstairs.

In the living room, Melanie is sitting in an oversized leather armchair. She looks up when she hears us coming down the stairs.

"Momma, look!" Kat says, showing Melanie the chessboard. "Alice and I did this puzzle together. Can you tell me how many squares there are?" Kat looks at me with a smile knowing that her mom is going to say...

"Sixty-four?"

"Nope! Look." Kat is showing her all the different sizes of squares, explaining as she goes. I am so proud of her and excited that she's excited.

"That's so cool, Kat. Did you figure this out on your own?" Melanie asks.

"Alice helped me."

"Yeah, but you did most of the work," I say to Kat.

With a smile on her face, Melanie looks at me. "Thanks so much for showing her this. How cool."

"You're welcome. I hope you don't mind that we did this," I say, worried that we didn't spend time on her homework or doing regular math practice.

"Not at all. This is great!

"Well, I should get going and leave you to the rest of your Saturday." Melanie gets up and follows me through the kitchen. I stop in the front entryway as she opens the front door for me.

"Alice, thank you again. She's getting so much out of working with you."

"You're welcome. It's my pleasure."

"If you want to bring other activities like the chessboard, we'd love to see her doing more creative things with math. I know she gets a little bored in class," she says. "I would love to see her have the positive relationship that I had with it. I try to show her things and I know she really likes the engineering set. Maybe you could incorporate things like that?"

"Wow, yes! I would love to. I had a lot of fun working on her Rube Goldberg machine. I tried to tell her that there was a lot of mathematical thinking that goes into a design like that. I'm not sure she was totally convinced, though."

"I love that you tried to show her. To be honest, I don't need her to be great at math, I just want her to like it."

"That's so great! I want that too." I'm amazed to hear someone say this because I know how much pressure there is for kids to do well in school and get good grades. I would love to see Kat doing more creative things with math.

"Well, again, we'd love for you to do more stuff like this with her. I try, but she isn't always that open to working with her mom. You know how girls at this age can be. I'm just not cool enough, I suppose."

"I wouldn't go that far," I say, trying to show Melanie that I thought she was pretty cool. "Okay, then, I'll try to come up with some ideas and I'll see you guys next week."

"Thanks so much. Have a great weekend!"

I have the same excited energy that I had after Jane's class when we worked in groups and made our presentations. Sure, that part wasn't the highlight, but I was able to use math creatively. Kat's engagement was so different today. When she does her homework, she pays attention and she's focused, but her eyes just lit up during the chessboard activity. She was talking and asking questions. What a great change of pace! Now I need to come up with some other things to do. I was certainly excited talking to Melanie. I just hope that I have the time to plan things like this and that I find cool things for Kat to work on.

Later that night, I meet Miranda for drinks at *The Grass Skirt*. We haven't been here in a while and it's packed tonight. Once we get our drinks Miranda and

I shuffle through the tables to snag the last two empty seats in the corner.

"Wow, I've never seen it this busy," I tell Miranda while wiping down the table with the napkin that came with my manhattan."

"I know! Maybe we should start spreading bad word of mouth so we can always get a table."

"I don't want that on my conscience, but you go right ahead."

Miranda sets her drink down on the table and slings her bag over the back of her chair. "So, you were telling me about the chessboard?"

"Oh, right. Miranda, it was amazing. I had the best time showing Kat the chessboard activity from the book. Remember, I was telling you about it?"

"Yeah, the squares."

"Right, well, Kat was so excited that she wanted to show her mom and when I was leaving, Melanie asked if I could do more things like that. Like, plan some fun math activities to do during tutoring."

"Wow, Alice, that's pretty cool. Are you still doing her homework with her?"

"I guess so. I thought I would split the session in half. Miranda, seriously, you should have seen the difference in the way she was working. Her homework is so boring, but she lit up when we did the chessboard thing."

"What kind of homework is she getting?"

"Just worksheets with endless practice problems. Sometimes she'll do a few problems and once she understands it she asks if she has to finish the whole page. I tell her yes, even though it's not fun watching her do problem after problem. They're almost all the same."

"Oh, is it not as 'fun' as Jane describing conjecture?" Miranda, laughs, reminding me of how much I enjoyed that lesson in class.

"I mean, nothing is as fun as that!" I say. "Seriously though, I'm looking forward to finding more cool activities for her."

"What happened with the summer camp job?"

"Oh yeah! I can't believe I didn't tell you," I say. "I talked to Emma, the owner of the company, and she's looking to expand their programming to other locations. She'll basically train me and show me what to do. I just have to set it up and run it."

"Whoa! That's awesome."

"I know! I'm kind of nervous though. I've never done anything like this before. I've worked with kids at different jobs, but I've never run a camp on my own like this. It's a little scary."

"It sounds really cool though."

"Yeah, it does." Then I get an idea. "Actually, would you be interested in helping me?"

"I don't know," Miranda says. "Yeah, wow, I'll definitely think about it. What would I have to do?"

"I guess just help the girls with the activities. I would give the instructions and you would be sort of my assistant."

"Hmm, I don't know how I feel about working for you," Miranda says with a laugh.

"Well, it would be fun working together and I think it's a great program. I can't believe there's a math camp designed just for girls. It seems too good to be true."

After working with Kat, these camps seemed like the perfect idea. Girls need an outlet like this so that they can appreciate math. What a difference it was today with Kat. I hope the summer program is as much fun as the experience was today. I would do this forever if I could make math fun.

12

As the nights get longer and the sun warms the porch until late in the evening, Cullen and I can sit outside after dinner and relax. I can hear the neighborhood noise start to fade as kids return home from their outdoor play. Tonight is the first time we're able to dust off our portable grill from the garage. I love the smokey smell and the charred taste of barbecued sausages and corn on the cob.

Cullen pulls the cover down on the grill to let the coals cool for the night. "How's the planning coming for your summer camps?" he asks.

"Good. I've been talking to Emma a lot and she's basically showing me everything I need to do to set up the camps. I'm still looking for a location and she's sending me the program activities this week. It's all happening so fast but I'm excited."

"That's so cool that you're doing that." Cullen returns to the porch and sits next to me. "What did Miranda decide about helping you?"

"She says she's in!" I tell him. I was so excited and also relieved to have my close friend along for the ride. "I think it's gonna be a lot of work but a lot of fun, at least for now."

Cullen looks puzzled. "What do you mean?"

"Well, I can't do it long-term because it's only a summer job. I should be trying to find something full-time. We need the money." My excitement drops a bit when I think about the fact that this is only possible for the summer and I'll still need to find something permanent.

"We're okay for now," Cullen tried to reassure me. "This sounds like it's going to be good money and then after the summer you can look for something else."

"I guess so."

"Honey, don't worry too much about that now. We'll figure it out."

"I know. I'm gonna worry a little though if that's okay."

Cullen laughs. "Sure, go ahead."

As the sun begins to fade I start to feel the cool night air brush against my skin. Cullen grabs our dishes and heads inside, leaving me to think about the next couple of months. At least I have plans for after graduation, which is amazing, but without a regular job, I'm worried that my degree isn't gonna get me where I want to go. I know there's work as a tutor but that isn't exactly paying the bills.

Back in the house, Cullen is putting away our dinner leftovers. "So, I talked to Kristen today."

"Oh yeah? How's she doing?" I ask.

"Good, we were discussing plans for her trip."

"Is that four weeks away?" I ask, looking at the calendar. "No, wait. It's three. Man, I'm gonna be so busy finishing finals and getting ready for graduation."

"I know. Kristen doesn't have the best timing."

"No, it's fine. Besides, she's coming for a work conference. She can't help it."

"I guess." Cullen and Kristen didn't always get along that well. I was hoping for a fun visit, even though she was only staying for a few days.

"Is there anything she wants to do when she's here?"

"Not really. We'll probably just hang out at the house. I'm sure she'd like to spend some quality time with Rick Moranis," he says looking down at his fat little buddy. "You'd like that, right Ricky?"

At school on Wednesday there's a banner in the hallway that reads "Congrats, Seniors! Happy Finals Week!" I can't believe it's all coming to an end. Miranda wanted to meet today to study before the final. She was already in our usual study corner in the Brandford Hall study lounge when I arrived.

"Hey, Alice!" she says as soon as she sees me. Miranda seems to be in a good mood today despite the fact that we have a final in less than two hours. "I can't believe this is our last week!"

"I know! It's so surreal," I tell her. "When is the final for your other class?"

"Tomorrow afternoon," she says.

"Okay, then, we definitely need to go out on

Friday night and celebrate."

"Absolutely. I suppose the boys can come too," she says sarcastically. Of course, we couldn't celebrate without thanking them for all their support over these last few years.

"Sure, but this is our night. All music talk must be kept to a minimum!" I mirror Miranda's good mood thinking about how the pressure is almost over. It's been a long road with so many ups and downs. I can't recall how many sleepless nights or near panic attacks I've had trying to get homework assignments done. "Seriously though, Miranda, I'm so lucky that I met you and had someone to work with all these years. I don't know if I would have gotten through the program without you."

"Aww, back at you!"

My backpack feels so much lighter today, which is a nice change. It's as if the weight school has literally been released. Taking out my notebook I look around the study hall. It's almost packed today with students. Most people have their heads down and they're focusing on their work. You can feel the tension so much more during finals week.

"I wonder why they made this room so drab," I say to Miranda.

She looks around the room. "What do you mean?"

"I dunno. It's very uninspiring. Grey walls, all the tables and chairs are brown or muted colors. It doesn't make you feel too happy to be in here."

"Well, most people aren't!" she informs me.

132

"They're studying, not having a party."

I know, but if there were brighter colors in here, it might make people happier. Color can affect your mood."

"Yeah, that's true."

"Like your colored pens. Your notes make me happier."

"Are you serious?" Miranda asks.

"Yeah, I mean, probably because that's how we met."

Miranda scrunches up her face with a questioning look. "Huh?"

"Didn't I ever tell you this? When we met on the first day of class, I was mesmerized by all of your colored pens and your system for taking notes. I thought you were really interesting, and I wanted to meet you."

"You never told me that! Alice, that's hilarious!"

"Well, now you know that your pens brought us together."

"I thought you just wanted another girl to talk to."

"Well, yeah, that's true," I say. "I mean, I guess if it wasn't for those pens, I would have no interest in being your friend."

Miranda laughs. "Well, I'm glad that I'm obsessed with colored pens, for the sake of our friendship."

"Me too," I tell her. We don't have long to study but it's nice keeping this tradition alive. Being with Miranda helps to relax me before the final and since I prepared so much, I'm not that worried.

Walking into Jane's class is an exhilarating feeling. Our final starts at ten o'clock. By 11:30 A.M I will be done with school. Done! I can't believe it's almost here. I haven't worked so hard for anything in my life. One more final and then I'll have a degree in mathematics. Wow! That hasn't sunk in yet. I wasn't sure I'd ever go to college and now I have a degree in math. That's incredible! I have to admit, once I get my diploma and hang it on the wall, I will be so proud of this accomplishment.

"Good morning," Jane says. She's wearing a bright yellow shirt today, which for some reason makes me smile. She's so bright and cheerful. I wonder if this was a conscious decision to lighten the mood, although most people seem happy today. Students don't seem to be too panicked. Usually, I see a lot of people hunched over the desks and studying as much as they can in the last few minutes they have left before a test. Today there's a calmness in the air. It's actually a little eerie. I hope this isn't the calm before the storm.

Jane begins to hand out the tests and as they are passed down the rows of desks, students who have never talked to each other in all these weeks together are wishing each other good luck. A lot of time the math program can feel competitive because we are all aware that the job market is only going to take some of us, and we have to rise above the rest. It's nice to see the camaraderie today instead. I want to kiss this test and say goodbye. Or, rather, say hello to no more tests, no more homework, and no more worrying about grades and assignments. Hello, future! Here I come.

Flipping through the test pages I'm relieved to see that the questions are what I predicted. Jane gave us a review packet and Miranda and I worked through all the problems again this morning. There are eight questions and I get through them without too much trouble. The adrenaline is pumping through my veins. This is it. I'm almost done!

I look at the clock and see that I still have plenty of time left. After I finish the last problem I go back to the beginning and check over my work. I can't believe this is it. I don't have to take any more tests. Once the final is over, I feel an enormous weight being lifted off my shoulders. As soon as I'm finished, I pack up my things, grab my test, and walk to the front of the class where Jane is sitting at her desk. I can't help myself but give her a huge smile as I had in my test papers. I thank her for a wonderful class and say good-bye.

"We did it!" I say to Miranda who's waiting in the hallway as she always does. She has a huge smile on her face and I can tell that she's as grateful as I am that we made it through.

Miranda puts her arms around me.

"Congratulations, Alice! You're done with school!"

"Oh man, Miranda, you have no idea how happy I am." It still hasn't hit me yet that this is all over. I did it.

"Let's celebrate! How about a cup of coffee?"

Miranda suggests.

"Sounds good," I say.

At the coffee cart where we have spent so many afternoons getting a pick-me-up after a long class, it's so nice to finally be here without any classes to worry about. I can't wait to celebrate.

13

"What time are we meeting them tonight?" Cullen asks. Rick Moranis is settled in on his lap and I can tell that he is actually asking how much couch time he has left.

"Miranda said they're gonna be there around eight-thirty. We should leave in about twenty minutes." I'm so thrilled to celebrate graduating and the end of all this hard work. We're meeting Miranda and Jacob at *The Grass Skirt*, which has become our regular hangout. It seemed fitting to reminisce where we spent a lot of nights venting about class and talking about our hopes for the future.

"Should I get dressed up?" asks Cullen.

"That would be nice. I know it's kind of a dive bar, but it's a big night. I think I'm gonna wear my new purple skirt."

"Okay. I'll put on something nice." Cullen tries to stand up but as soon as he pulls Rick Moranis off his lap he crawls right back on. "Sorry, buddy. I have to get ready."

It's fun to get dressed up and go out with Miranda and Jacob. We haven't all hung out together since our game night a few months ago. I'm excited to be out on the town with my guy, celebrating this huge achievement.

Coming out of the bathroom I see Cullen standing near the front door. He's wearing a dress shirt and dark jeans and as he turns, he reveals his purple tie, picked out to match my skirt.

"Oh, honey. That's so sweet. Now we match."

"Well, I want people to know we're together," he says. "I'm so proud of you." He reaches out to give me a hug and kisses me gently on the cheek. I'm actually choked up because it hits me all at once. Someone recognizes me and what I've accomplished. This is going to be a wonderful night.

When we arrive, Miranda and Jacob are already there and sitting at a large arched booth near the front door. There's a lot of noise and commotion inside. Part of me wants to announce that we've arrived and have everyone join us in the festivities.

"Hey guys," I say as we join them at the table. They already have a head start on drinks. I look to Cullen. "Should we grab a drink before we settle in?"

"I'll go up. Manhattan?"

"Yes, please!" I say and join our friends at the table.

Miranda notices Cullen's tie as he turns towards the bar. "You guys match. How cute!"

"Yes, we're so adorable," I reply.

"Hey, Alice. Congratulations," says Jacob.

"Thanks! I still can't believe it's over. It hasn't hit me yet."

"Me neither," adds Miranda.

"So, Miranda's been telling me about camp," Jacob says. "Are you excited?"

"Yes, but I'm nervous too," I say. "It's gonna be fun though" I turn to Mirnada. "Oh, I found a location. The Helping Hands Community Center has a room available. Emma is gonna set up the camp registration for us this week."

"Oh god, it's actually real," she says. "That's exciting!"

"Yeah! It's just a few weeks away. I hope we get enough girls signed up. Emma says her camps are always full, but I don't know how well we're gonna do. I mean, this is the first time she's letting people run camps out of state."

"Or, we might get too many girls, and then we'd be in over our heads!"

"Very true."

Cullen comes back with our drinks and slides into the booth next to me.

"Hey, man," Jacob nods to him. "Did you check out that band I was telling you about?"

"Oh no, here we go," I say to Miranda.

"Okay, okay. Sorry," says Cullen, lifting his glass. "Here's to two amazing women. Congratulations!"

"To Miranda and Alice," adds Jacob, lifting his bottle of beer and clinking our glasses. "So proud of you both."

I'm proud of us too. Looking at Miranda I start to remember these last four years and all the time we spent together. It's been quite a journey of ups and downs. I'm so happy to have an amazing support system of both her and Cullen. This means so much to me to be here right now with these people. Even though it's been a long road, I feel as if everything is just beginning.

We were out late last night and I'm sort of tired when I get to Kat's house. I try to keep my energy up when I'm with her, which normally isn't too hard, but today it's a little more challenging.

"Hi Kat," I say when she opens the door. "How are you today?"

"Okay." Her voice is soft, and she doesn't have her usual bouncy energy.

"Just okay?" I ask.

"Yes," she responds.

"What's the matter?"

"We found out that I have Mr. Stevenson next year for math and everyone says he's really mean."

"Oh, well, I'm sure he can't be that bad."

"No, he is," she informs me. "My friend Jenny's sister had him for sixth grade and she said he yelled a lot and she hated his class."

"Oh no. Well, I wouldn't worry about it too much. You have the whole summer to have fun. Go in with an open mind. He might surprise you."

Looking up at me she asks, "are you still gonna

be my tutor next year?"

"Oh, I dunno," I say. I hadn't actually thought about it but I don't want Kat to worry that I won't be here. "Probably."

"Alice, you have to." She seems panicked. "I won't be able to do math without you."

"Oh, Kat. Let me just say that you're an incredible young lady. You're so creative and you have a wonderful mind. Don't let anyone make you think that you can't do math, and don't think that about yourself because I've seen you do such great work."

"I guess so," she says.

"I know so." Since it's the last week of school for Kat, she doesn't have any homework again, which is actually a nice change of pace. I'm not in the mood to do a worksheet, especially now that I'm done with homework. "Should we continue working on your business plan?"

Last week she told me that she was making all-natural soaps and wanted to give them to her friends. We started talking about turning this into a small business and I told her about all the math that she would use. I figured this would be a fun summer project and I encouraged her to run a table outside to see if she could sell some of her soaps.

"Yeah, I made some more soaps this week and tried different shapes. Momma bought me some new molds. Do you wanna see?"

"Of course! Let's go look." In her room, Kat has all of her supplies including ingredients, molds, and a variety of soaps in different shapes and colors. "I like these pink ones," I tell her, picking one up to smell it. "Oh, I thought this might smell like something pink. Have you thought about scents?"

"No, I didn't think about that." She holds one of the pink soaps. "What should this one be?"

I think for a moment. "How about bubblegum, or watermelon? Think of some pink things. You want the smell to match the color."

"Bubblegum sounds good! I wonder if I can get oils or something to put in the pink batches."

"This should be your next step. Start to develop different scents to match the colors."

"Okay, let's do that!" Kat gets right to work. She pulls out her business plan that we started last week and writes down all the colors she has so far. She is very organized and methodical, which is how I know she's cut out to excel at math. I love seeing the way her mind works.

After making her list, she is deciding on the different scents, asking my opinion on each one. It takes about fifteen minutes and she has her product list complete.

"So, you have different sizes too." I pick up one of the flower-shaped soaps that she made with her new molds. "Are you going to charge more for these?"

"Hmm." She thinks for a minute. "I think I'll do five dollars for that one."

"That sounds good. Let's make a list of the different sizes and organize them by price." Her business idea is coming together, and I'm so impressed with the amount of work she's put in so far. She's very committed to everything she does, and I admire her for that. When she was working on her Rube Goldberg machine she never gave up. She kept plugging away, making modifications, and problem-solving until she got it right.

"Kat, this looks great so far. I have to say, I'm really impressed with your work. I mean, you took a hobby and you're trying to make something more with it. It's very cool." I start to wonder if there are other girls who are doing things like this. It would be amazing to get some friends to also showcase their creativity and make something to sell.

"So, Kat, do you think you have friends that would like to do this with you? Maybe they can make something to sell and you can run the table together?"

"Oh yeah! My friend Abby makes jewelry. She might want to do this too."

"You should talk to her about it," I tell her. "Show her all the work you've put in so far. You could teach her."

"Yeah! I could do that when she comes over tomorrow."

"That sounds like a great idea!"

"Do you think she could also come over next Saturday when you're here and we could do this together?"

It sounds like a good idea, but I don't know if that fits into our arrangement. "Well, I'm not sure," I say. "Your mom hired me as a tutor and, ya know, she's paying me for this hour. I don't know if your friend can join us."

It did sound like a fun idea, but I was worried about what this was turning into. Technically I was Kat's tutor and I was getting paid just to work with her alone. Now we were working on a project. I'm not even sure what this job is right now. I don't want this to seem like glorified babysitting. We weren't even working on her homework anymore. Was I even still her tutor?

On the way to pick up Kristen from the airport, Cullen and I are trying to analyze this new situation I had with Kat. "It sounds like it's getting complicated," he says.

"I know. I feel like I would have to charge the other parent, right?" I ask.

"I would think so. I mean, if you're working with two of them, then you should get paid by both families."

"It's tricky though. If you think about it like I'm getting paid for an hour of my time, then that's still the same."

"Well, you have to decide and be firm with them," Cullen says. "I don't want you to do more work and not get compensated."

"Me neither. I'll think about it. Actually, this business plan would be a good idea to do at a summer camp."

"Oh yeah, that would be perfect. Can you do that?"

"No, I have to stick with Emma's program. She has it all detailed and there's no flexibility."

"Oh, that's too bad."

Getting to the airport I'm so excited to see Kristen. Not only that, but I love coming to the airport because it's so heart-warming to see the joy on people's faces when their loved ones get off the plane. The reactions are all so different and it's fun to see who gets emotional. As we're waiting, we see a woman, probably in her 30s, who actually screams when she sees her friend. She jumps up and it scares me for a second, but they run over and give each other a big hug and it is so beautiful. There's also a guy around my age waiting with a bouquet of yellow roses. Maybe he's waiting for his long-lost love who is returning from an overseas trip. I wonder if he's gonna get down on one knee and propose in front of all these strangers. That would be a sight to see! I've never witnessed a proposal before.

When I was in high school my friends and I would sometimes come to the airport to people-watch and walk around the little touristy shops. We didn't do it often, but I liked getting a small, voyeuristic view into people's relationships.

Kristen's plane is landing now. I can't wait to see her! I might be more excited than Cullen is. When she gets to the gate she looks like a movie star.

"Kristen! You're here! I'm so happy to see you." I run over and put my arms around her. I wonder how many people are watching us and getting a bit of joy from observing how happy we are to see each other.

145

"Hey, sis," Cullen says, grabbing her bags and hugging her with one arm. "How was your flight?"

"Not bad, actually. My company paid for a seat in business class. I'm an upscale business-type person after all," she says. Of course she's exaggerating, but Kristen does have a pretty cool job. She's been working for a local high school in Palo Alto since she got her Master's. They recently promoted her to the position of Program Director. She does a lot of event planning and helps to develop after school programs for at-risk youth.

"Do you have more bags?" Cullen asks.

"Yes, two more."

"You're only staying for a few days. What in the world did you bring?"

"You know me. I never travel light."

Cullen and I are always amazed at how much people can pack for a short trip. We always share a carry-on, even if we're vacationing for a whole week. It's our traveling mission to bring as little as possible.

"So, Alice. Tell me what you've been up to." Kristen turns back to me from the front seat of the car. "How was graduation?"

"It was so great. My family came and we went out for dinner after the ceremony. It was nice being with them. The ceremony didn't mean that much to me though. I mean, I was so excited to graduate, but it's not like high school where you know everyone in the graduating class. In college, you're more anonymous."

"That's exciting though! I'm so happy for you. I'm just sorry I couldn't be here for it."

"That's okay. It's nice that you're here now." I give her a smile.

"At least you think so," she says, then turns to Cullen. "I don't know how excited my brother is." She gives him a push on the arm.

"What? I didn't say anything."

"Do you see what I have to put up with? Growing up he was the same way. Never happy to see his sister."

"It's because you're older and I never liked any of your snotty friends," he informs her.

"Oh, is that why? Mmm-hmm." Kristen doesn't seem convinced.

Cullen seems very ready to change the subject. "Babe, tell Kristen about Kat. Maybe she can give you some insight. She works with a lot of kids and families."

"What's going on? Who's Kat?" she asks.

"Oh, it's this girl in our neighborhood. I started working with her as a math tutor. I started bringing her activities to do because she's bored with doing worksheets and stuff. Anyway, she's done with school and I told her over the summer break we could work on a project that uses math."

"How exciting! What are you working on?"

"She makes soaps and I thought it would be fun if she designed a little business and tried to sell them."

Kristen's face lights up when she hears this. "That's a cool idea."

"Yeah, she's been really into it. I suggested getting her friend involved and she asked if I would work with them together. Now I don't know if I should ask for more money. You know, maybe the other parent should pay for our time together? It feels a little uncomfortable."

"Oh Alice, you're too nice. I think that's great what you're doing but you have to watch out for yourself. I mean, is this something you want to keep doing?"

"Actually, I just got a summer job running math camps for girls."

"Oh, that's perfect then! It sounds like you could take this idea and run with it."

"What do you mean?" I ask.

"Well, if you learn some math activities that would appeal to girls you could run them in your neighborhood. It sounds like you might already have a few girls that would be interested."

"I guess that's true. I don't know if I could run my own program though."

"Why not?" she asks.

"It just seems like a lot of work. This company that I'm working with has it all planned out already."

"But you have your own ideas," Cullen says. "It sounds like there's more you can do."

Kristen turns to Cullen and then back at me. "You really should think about it," she says. "I can help you design a program. Heck, that's what I do for a living!"

Was she serious? I couldn't start my own business. Could I?

Back at the house, Kristen and I settle in on the porch for a while, even though it's already late in the evening. "Tell me more about Kat," Kristen says. Cullen is already in bed, but we wanted to stay outside a little longer and talk.

"Oh man, where do I start? She's such an awesome girl. She lives down the street. My neighbor Daisy introduced me to her mom just after they moved in earlier this year. Kat has a lot of energy and she's really creative."

"How's she doing in math?"

"Good, I mean, I know she can do it but she has a hard time because she gets bored and loses focus. She's really worried about next year because, apparently, she has a teacher that's 'mean'. I've been helping her with her homework though and she's doing great."

"So then, you're doing these projects too?" asks Kristen.

"Yeah, we started a few weeks ago. I was incorporating more creative activities and we started the business plan project for her to do over the summer."

"Alice, that's so cool," Kristen says. "I think you're offering a unique gift to her. Students have such a hard time in math and they almost never like it. What you're doing is really needed."

"Yeah, like with the camps I'm doing this summer. I couldn't believe this was even out there and I didn't know about it. I wish I had something like that when I was a kid. I might have stuck with math and not shied away from it when I was in middle school."

149

Doing a little research, there were a couple of camps like this for girls, but they were few and far between. It makes me think about the gender divide in math. Of course, I lived it, but it's unfortunate that there must be programs designed specifically for girls. It makes me wonder why girls don't seem to like math. There seems to be a need for camps like these, but I wonder if girls are that excited to join. It's funny. The camps are designed to get girls interested in math, but if they're not interested, they won't want to come to camp. You hear the words 'math camp' and it must sound intimidating. I hope our camps go well though. Miranda and I have been prepping but I'm worried that I can't make mathematics as much fun as I think it is.

Part Three

14

My nerves are getting the best of me. Miranda and I are meeting at the community center at 9:00 A.M to set up for camp. This is our first day and I honestly have no idea what to expect. Even though the whole day is planned out and scheduled, you never know what's gonna happen.

"Hey! Are you ready?" I ask Miranda as she's getting out of her car.

"As ready as I'll ever be," she says. "Here, let me help you with that." I hand her a box of supplies and we walk into the community center doors, heading upstairs to the classroom I've reserved for the week. I checked out the room last week to see the layout. It wasn't so scary at the time, but now it's a room that is about to be full of girls who expect me to know what I'm doing.

The room is large and open with tall windows at the far end. There's a small counter and sink along the front wall and cabinets underneath for storage. Right away, Miranda and I start setting up the long folding tables that are in the hallway for visitors to use. The folding chairs are in a closet and Miranda and I work together to set up fifteen, making small groups around the tables for the girls to sit together as they work.

"Can you set these out?" I ask Miranda. I have a box of paper and pencils and the company's workbooks that Emma sent to me.

"Sure."

"Oh my gosh, we only have twenty minutes. I'm so nervous," I say.

"We got this. Don't worry, Alice. Whatever happens, happens."

A few minutes after nine-thirty our first camper arrives. A little shy, she's clinging to the back of her mom's shirt as she hides behind her.

"Good morning!" I say to them, putting on my customer service smile.

"Hi. This is Sofia," the woman informs me. "And I'm Heather." She reaches out to shake my hand and tries to get Sofia to come out from hiding.

"Hi, Heather," I say to her. "Good morning, Sofia. My name is Alice and I'm the instructor for this camp. This is Miranda."

"Hi." Sophia's voice is quiet and she's looking around the room trying to take it all in.

"Would you like to pick a seat?" I look to her mom for support. "Your mom can sit with you until the others get here if you'd like."

"Sofia, where would you like to sit?" Heather asks.

"You have your pick," Miranda tells her. "Which is the best seat in the house?"

Tentatively, Sofia picks a seat near the window and her mom joins her at the table.

"If you'd like to pick one of the workbooks on the table, that will be your camper notebook for the week," I tell them. "You can start filling out the 'About Me' page. We'll talk about that when the others get here." Heather hands her one of the workbooks and they begin flipping through it. Sofia grabs a pencil and starts writing in the book. As soon as she's settled in a few other girls arrive. One by one we get them checked in and seated at a table. The room is so quiet that it adds to the awkwardness. Miranda and I are doing our best to engage with the girls, but I can tell that they're nervous because they aren't interacting too much.

Once all fifteen girls are in and settled it's time to start. Showtime! I better put on my confidence hat or they're gonna know that I have no idea what I'm doing.

"Good morning, girls! My name is Alice and I'm gonna be your camp instructor for the whole week. This is Miranda and she'll be here to help with anything you need." The words are coming out as if I've done this one hundred times. I'm still nervous, but once I get up here and start talking it starts to melt away. After all the work of planning over the last few weeks, we're finally here. It's a little surreal.

We have an activity in the morning and the girls are starting to talk more. Miranda and I are trying to be bubbly and energetic, which can be a stretch for me. I don't think I've talked this much in an entire day my whole life.

Overall, the day is going well. We made it to lunch without any problems and it's nice to take a break and sit outside. The grass is a bit damp, but it's a beautiful, sunny day. Some girls are sitting in the shade, but Miranda and I love the heat and are warming ourselves in the hot sun.

"Can you open this for me?" Karie, one of the more outgoing girls of the group, hands me one of those yogurt tubes that are almost impossible to open without getting it all over your hands.

"Sure," I say, tearing it open. The inevitable pink goo spills out of the top. "Here you go." Karie heads back to her small group who's sitting at the edge of the lawn near a paved walkway. They just met this morning, but it looks like there are some girls who are starting to make friends.

"Thanks so much for helping me with this camp," I say to Miranda. "It's going well, right?"

"Yeah, it seems like the girls are enjoying it, but it's hard to tell."

"I know. They're so quiet. But, it's the first day. It must be awkward walking into a new camp where you don't know anybody."

"For sure."

By the end of the day, I'm tired but so happy that we made it through. Now I don't have to worry because I know what to expect. It's so much fun getting to know the girls and seeing how they approach a math problem. I hope that they can get stronger in math and really see the value in it. The activities that we're doing combine art and math. The goal is to find a way for girls to have fun with math, but I'd love to see a camp where they get to work on real-world problems and see how math is used every day. Too often in schools students are simply doing calculations and working on practice problems. It doesn't seem like kids can effectively use math.

One of the moms said something pretty shocking today. She was worried that her daughter was starting to not like math, mostly because they have timed multiplication tests at school which are very stressful. She has to answer fifty problems in four minutes! This woman was telling me about her experience with the same type of tests and when she was her daughter's age they had timed tests at the end of the school year. If you were one of the lucky students to complete the test in time, you were able to get ice cream as your reward. Sadly, she didn't make it in time and had to watch her friends get a treat for completing the test quickly. Not only was she negatively affected by this, but it completely sent the message that speed is important in math. She was choked up telling me this story and it made me realize how traumatized people can be by math. What is happening in our schools that nurtures math anxiety? It really breaks my heart.

I'm worried that Kat is going to have a hard time

next year with her new teacher. She's already thinking she's not gonna like him. Also, if he is as mean as she thinks he's going to be, she might have a hard time asking for help in class. It makes me want to keep tutoring her, but I can't be her tutor for life. At some point, things have to get better in school. That's where it starts.

I've been thinking more about continuing with a math program for girls. After talking with Kristen during her visit, I was inspired to keep going with camps like I'm running now. Unfortunately with this summer job, I'm at the mercy of someone else and I don't have the creative freedom to come up with my own activities. I'd like to tailor the program to the needs of the girls as I do with Kat.

At the end of the week, Miranda and I decided to unwind on her front porch and have a few drinks. It's fun discussing the week and what we thought went well and what we can do better.

"I liked the activity where the girls were discovering pi by using the string to measure the diameter and seeing how many times it went around the circle," Miranda tells me.

"Me too! I don't know that I've ever really thought about that connection. I mean, I know the formula that I learned in school for the circumference, but that visual made so much more sense."

"Why don't we see more interactive stuff like

that in schools?"

"I don't know. We do so much math on paper. It's like when I work with Kat. It's worksheet after worksheet. I'm so bored. Also, she doesn't get the opportunity to discover anything for herself or discuss an idea." I grab the bottle of wine off the porch railing and refill my glass. "Remember that day in Jane's class where we worked in groups and I ended up presenting? That day was so much fun. I mean, Jane is a great teacher, but we didn't have to just listen to her and take notes. We were actively participating. I wish all math classes were like that."

"Seriously," Miranda says. "I went through so many of our courses in college where I could do the work on a test, but honestly, I don't know that I can use half of the math we learned."

"Same here. It's sad actually. We spent so much time struggling and for what? This is why I worried about getting a job. Actually, I'm still worried. I don't know what I can do with my degree. Maybe that's why I always got asked if I was gonna be a teacher. I mean, what else could I do?"

"I know it feels that way, but we have a lot of options."

"I want things to change," I say. Two glasses of wine and I'm in a math rant. "I want people to see how valuable math is and I want it to start in schools. It's no wonder why people hate math so much."

"Have you ever gone to a party or been with a

group of people and when you say you like math or that you're a math major, they wince?" Miranda asks. "Or, when you talk about math with someone they very readily say, 'I hate math'?"

"Yes! That happens all the time! It feels like the only subject where that happens. No one ever says, 'I hate history, yuck!'."

Miranda laughs. "I know, can you imagine?"

Talking with Miranda about math is usually an endless conversation. It's funny though, we don't actually talk about mathematical ideas. We vent about math education and other people's perception of math. I wish I didn't love something that so many people hate.

"This week was fun though," I say. "The girls were great. You know, Kristen and I were talking, and she thinks I should run my own camps."

"Really? What do you mean?"

"Basically, take this idea and run with it. This is an amazing opportunity, and I love what they're doing, but I want to design my own camps. There's a real need for programs like this."

"Wow, that's huge. Are you thinking about it?"

"Maybe, yeah. I could start planning and run my own camps next year. Emma has taught me so much already. I mean, I don't know how to run a business exactly, but I could probably learn."

"That's so cool, Alice. I think that's a great idea."

I'm not sure if it's the wine talking or if this idea is worth exploring. I've learned how to run the camps and coming up with the curriculum sounds like a lot of fun. I've always wanted to run my own business someday, and this is something I'm deeply passionate about. Being a woman in math is a good catalyst for designing a math program for girls.

15

I'm still working with Kat, but now that I'm also running camps, it's harder to give up my time on Saturdays. I told Melanie that I could finish our small business project, but after that, I would have to take a break.

"Are you going to be available in the fall?" Melanie asks. "Kat is worried about her new teacher."

"Oh, yeah she told me." I'm nervous about making the commitment but I'm torn because I want to help her. "I should be available, but to be honest, I'm thinking about starting my own business."

"Wow! That's incredible. What type of business?"

"Actually, I'd like to run math camps for girls, sort of like I'm doing now, but this way I can design my own activities."

"That's so great. I know Kat would love to join," says Melanie. "We couldn't make it work this summer, but she would love to keep working with you. I know she could use the tutoring help too, so please keep us in mind."

Thinking about helping Kat with her homework again seemed sort of dreadful now that I'm running camps. The weeks I spend with the girls are certainly a lot of work, but they are also so much fun. I get to see the girls talking about math and sharing ideas. I like seeing how creative they are. I guess that's why I was drawn to Kat in the first place. She's an energetic and spunky young girl and it's interesting to see her making things and problem-solving. It almost feels like tutoring isn't the right fit for me anymore.

"Also," Melanie adds, "I was talking to her friend Abby's mom. They might also be looking for a tutor if you're interested." Just when I thought I was making my getaway.

"Oh, okay. I'll let you know. Certainly, if she wants to join us for the small business project I'm doing with Kat, or even my camps in the future, I'd love to see her."

"Well, I know Abby struggles with math. They might just want the tutoring help. But I'll let them know."

I'm beginning to wonder if my passion for alternative math projects are as desirable as I thought. Girls might just need help with their schoolwork. That's so frustrating though. How can I ever show girls how fascinating math can be if we're doing worksheets? I can't make that fun.

Walking home, Daisy is outside in her garden picking tomatoes off her vines. "Hi there, Alice. Would you like some tomatoes?" she asks.

"Sure, thanks." I'm still thinking about the business idea and feeling a little discouraged. Today's appointment with Kat was fun and I want that feeling to continue. On my way out, Melanie asked me if I had any workbooks that I could recommend for Kat to do during her summer break. I feel like I'm going in the wrong direction because she said she wanted Kat to like math. I don't know how she can like math if she's stuck doing workbooks.

"Are you doing okay?" Daisy must have picked up on my negative vibe.

"Yeah, okay I guess. I'm a little frustrated, that's all."

"Why? What's up?"

"It's kind of a long story."

"I have time. Do you wanna come in for some iced tea?"

I think for a minute and decide it might be nice to talk. "Sure, that sounds good."

I haven't been inside Daisy's house for a while. There's a sharp smell that I can't put my finger on. It's a mix between lavender and mint with a dash of curry. She has knick-knacks on most of the shelves and plants in macramé hangers in her kitchen.

"So, what's going on with you?" Daisy pulls out two tall, etched glasses from her kitchen cabinet. Her refrigerator is packed to the gills and it takes some shuffling and rearranging before she finds a pitcher of iced tea. As she's pouring me a glass, I tell her about the business idea and my work with Kat.

"I'm having a great time working with her, don't get me wrong, and Melanie is so great. I just don't know if I want to go back to tutoring her in the fall. The camps I'm doing now are so cool. I think a program like this would do well, but I'm not sure how on board parents are gonna be." I take a sip of iced tea, wiping the already formed condensation on the leg of my jeans. "But if girls don't like math, then they may not want to even come to a camp like this."

"But it sounds like the camp you're running is doing well."

"Yeah, that's because the company that organized it has a strong following and I think their name recognition helped. I would be starting from scratch."

Daisy looks at me with her sympathetic eyes. "Alice, if you're passionate about it and you stay true to what you want to do, others will follow."

"I guess that's true."

"What does Cullen say about it?"

"He's been supportive but I'm sure he's nervous. We have a mortgage to pay and starting a business can be risky. I don't even have start-up money. I would be doing this all from scratch."

"Could you start small and run a workshop or two, just to see how it goes? You said Kat and her friend might want to do something together."

"Yeah. I have a feeling a lot of girls would want to sign up with their friends."

"There you go. Start there and see what happens. Don't put too much pressure on yourself. You'll figure it out."

She was right, too. This didn't have to be a huge success right out of the gate. Let's be honest, most small businesses aren't. People say if you love what you do you never have to work a day in your life. I'm just worried about making enough money to survive.

"Thanks, Daisy. I know it's gonna take some time to figure it out, but I think it's a valuable concept. Starting small is a good idea." It was gonna take some networking and word of mouth to get this going. "Oh, hey. Susan was saying that her niece might need a tutor, but maybe this is something she would be interested in. Do you have Susan's number? I could reach out about the small business workshop and see if she'd like to join us. We might be able to get a small group going."

"That's a great idea! Yes, I have Susan's number. Do you want me to reach out and see if they're interested?"

"Definitely! Thanks so much," I say.

"Sure. How about I call her later and let you know what she says?"

"That sounds great. Well, I should be getting home. Cullen is expecting me. Thanks for the tea and the tomatoes."

"Anytime."

When I get home, Cullen is in the kitchen making lunch. The smell of food makes me wonder if our house has a smell that people notice when they walk in like I do at Daisy's house. I kind of hope not.

"Hey, hon. I stopped by Daisy's and she gave us these tomatoes," I said, handing him the small bag containing our neighborly gift.

"That's nice of her. How come you went to her house?"

"I saw her outside and we got to talking so she invited me in. I was telling her about the business, and I told her that Melanie wants me to keep tutoring Kat next year."

"Oh, that's good." He could tell by the look on my face that I wasn't too thrilled. "Isn't it?"

"Not if I want to start a business. I mean, I don't want to just help girls with their homework. That sounds bad," I say. "I just mean that I want to do something more fun and creative." I pick at Cullen's sliced veggies on the cutting board and help myself. "I was talking to Daisy and we're gonna try to get a group of girls together for the small business project."

"That's great. How many girls?" he asks.

"I'm not sure. Four or five at least. If they invite their friends, it could be more."

"Honey, that's great. It sounds like a good start to launching your business. I mean, if you decide to do that."

"I really want to. I just don't know if it's the best idea for us."

"Can you do more with the camps you're running now?"

"No, this is just a summer job. I wouldn't be able to do anything during the school year."

"Well, I think the small business workshop is probably a good way to start. If you need any help let me know."

"Thanks, baby. I will."

After a few hours online, I'm finding a lot of interesting math projects and different ideas that I could run as a workshop. I'm getting excited by the creative freedom of making my own projects. This is the fun part so, for now, I try and forget about the stress involved in launching a new business. There are so many possibilities! I still don't understand why teachers don't do more stuff like this, but I'm sure their hands are tied. Maybe the schools aren't ready to make modifications to their system. Deep down this is why I never wanted to teach. Kids have been learning math a certain way for so long. It's hard to change things.

16

I ended up getting nine girls to sign up for the small business workshop and I'm really happy with the turnout. This could have been a huge bust and I could have planned it all for nothing. I rented the same community center classroom that I had for camp and the girls are meeting me today to develop their business plans. I feel like this is a way for me to develop my own business since the idea is still in development.

"Good afternoon, girls. My name is Alice. Some of you know me because I tutor Kat. You might also know that she and I have been working on a business plan for her specialty soaps." It dawns on me that Kat might be able to explain her idea better than I can. "Actually, Kat, do you want to tell them what you have so far?"

Since Kat knows most of the girls, she seems confident talking to the group, but she is definitely a little more reserved than I have seen her previously.

"Well", she started, "Alice and I have been organizing my soaps by size, scent, and price. I have different sizes and shapes and we came up with prices I could sell them for." She showed the girls the samples that she brought, explaining how she made them and the different scents. "This pink one smells like bubblegum and it's five dollars, but I have bigger ones like the blue raspberry soap that is six dollars, and these are eight," she says, explaining her products to the group.

"That's great. Thank you, Kat," I say. I'm impressed and very proud of her. She's taking this very seriously and it's nice to see her dedication.

"So, first things first. You guys need to come up with a product idea. It has to be something that you can make on your own so that we can sell them at an event that Kat is hosting at her house. Feel free to talk with each other and brainstorm some ideas. You want to think about a few things." I make a list on the chalkboard so the girls can organize their ideas and start to make a plan. "If it's similar to something that already exists, you have to tell us why you think your product will sell over your competition. You also have to figure out if there is a need for your product. Once you get your idea, we'll talk about what it costs to make. That is called an expense, or what costs you money. Then you'll decide on a price for each item. When you subtract your expenses from your price, that is called your profit. This is the money you get to keep."

"Are we actually selling these?" asks one of the girls.

"Absolutely," I tell her.

"And we get to keep the money?"

"Yes, of course. If you work hard and come up with a unique idea, you can make money if it's something people want to buy."

"Awesome! I'm gonna save my money for a new art set," she says.

The girls get to work making a plan for their products. Some girls want to make things that might be too challenging to create in time, so I try to give them advice and see how they can make adjustments. There's so much laughter and creativity in the room. The girls seem to be really enjoying themselves and it's fun watching them work.

"How do we know how much to charge for our stuff?" asks Holly, Susan's niece. Holly is in fourth grade but she's very mature and I would have guessed she's in sixth. She had been working hard all day designing a beauty product line.

"Well, you have to think about what it costs to make, but also consider what someone might pay for it. If it's too cheap, they might not think it's good quality, but if it's too expensive, they might not want to pay that much."

"For the lotion, it will probably cost three dollars to make one bottle," she tells me. "Can I charge six?"

"Sure. That's called your markup. So, a markup is either the dollar amount or the percent that you charge over your expenses. So, this is a one hundred percent markup." She looks at me with little expression on her face and it seems like I'm not being clear. "Let's look at it another way. Tell me again, how much does it cost to make the bottle of lotion?"

"Three dollars," she says.

"And, how much are you charging?"

"Six dollars."

"Okay, so how much do you have to add to three to get to six?"

"Three."

"Great, so you add an extra three dollars to the cost, which was also three dollars. Since that's the same amount, that's one hundred percent. If you wanted a fifty percent markup, you would add half or fifty percent of three."

"Oh, I get it. Do I have to do one hundred percent?"

"No, you don't have to, but that could be how you figure out your prices. You wouldn't have to guess. You would use math!"

This is exactly what I was hoping to get out of this workshop. The girls are working so hard and I love hearing all their ideas. At pickup, one of the parents asked if I was going to do more events like this! That's a good sign.

Our second week of camp was a little more challenging. Today we had a camper that doesn't like math and didn't want to participate. When Miranda was asking her questions and trying to help her, she said that she didn't need math and that she had a calculator that would give her the answers. We explained that a calculator only works if you know what to put in. She didn't seem convinced.

"I didn't think about the girls that were forced to come here by their parents," Miranda tells me during lunch.

"I know. There are a few girls this week that clearly don't want to be here. It's actually a shame. I think they would enjoy it if they were more open to doing math, but they already have a chip on their shoulder."

"Yeah, I mean, when do kids start hating math? These girls are only in second grade. What a bummer."

"We're trying to make it fun, but they have to meet us halfway," I tell Miranda. "Oh, I didn't get a chance to tell you that Genny's mom told her that she was coming to an art camp. When they showed up and she found out it was a math camp she was really upset. That's why she's been so quiet today. She's really annoyed to be here."

"Man, why do parents do that?" Miranda rolls her eyes. "Of course she's gonna be miserable."

"I know. She didn't get a chance to prepare herself or find out what this was. Now she's probably gonna be upset all week unless we can convince her that math can actually be fun."

It's a reality check that we aren't going to succeed with every girl. When students don't like math it's hard to change their minds. How do we reach those girls?

It's also clear that the girls are at different skill levels, so some are working fast and some are behind. That's gonna be a challenge I'll have to face moving forward. The small business workshop went well because it was self-paced. I have to find a way for the girls to work at their own pace and not worry about how fast or slow others are working around them. Some of the girls say that they can't do math because they're slow. I want to show them that putting in the effort is how they'll succeed. It doesn't matter how fast they go. I wish schools weren't giving kids timed math tests. Now kids think that doing math quickly means you're good at it. Unfortunately, kids also think that if they do it slowly, they're bad at it.

"I'm starting to wonder who the camps are for, you know?" I ask Miranda.

"What do you mean?"

"Like, are we helping girls that already like math or girls that don't like it? It seems like there are so many different levels of engagement. It's hard to please everybody."

"Yeah, but you just have to do what feels right and see who comes along for the ride," she says.

"Oh, also, Lacy's mom said she loves the camp but asked if I tutored." I don't know how I feel about this. I mean, I'm flattered in some way, but these camps are far from tutoring. I don't know if her mom had made that connection.

"Oh, are you going to?" Miranda asks.

"I don't know. I'm torn because parents keep asking me to tutor, but I want to do more creative workshops and camps that show girls how useful math is. I want to take math off the page and into the real world. But then girls have to go back to school and do homework. I can't change that with one summer camp."

"That's tricky," Miranda says. "I think you have to pick a path that is the most rewarding for yourself. If you're passionate then you'll find families that believe in what you're doing. You can't please everybody."

"Clearly."

17

I've been thinking a lot about the business and who I actually want to help. What seemed so cut and dry is becoming a lot more complicated.

I can hear Cullen in the kitchen moving around bowls in the cabinets and shuffling pots and pans. It sounds like Sunday waffles are in my future.

"Good morning, love," I say, excited by the waffle iron I see on the counter and viscous brown goop in a bowl.

"Hey, you. I'm making breakfast! Coffee is ready."

"I see that. Thank you, my love," I say, grabbing a mug from the cabinet. "What inspired this?"

"I thought it would be nice for you to sleep in."

"Thanks, it was," I say, pouring myself a cup of coffee. "This week has been exhausting. I'm not physically tired but I'm mentally tired."

"I'll bet. How's camp going?"

"Not too bad. Actually, I started thinking about the girls that really need a math program like this. I'm considering starting a nonprofit."

"Whoa! That's huge," says Cullen.

"I know. It seems overwhelming, but I want to help families that can't afford math help and work with girls that need more opportunities. I feel weird that I'm making money off this. Like, I'm profiting from poor math education. When I tutor, it's families that have extra money that hire me. What about the girls that can't afford it?"

"Yeah. Wow, that's a really big thing. I don't even know where you would start. Obviously, you have to make some money, but I get what you're saying."

"Daisy mentioned that Susan ran a nonprofit for fifteen years. Her company provided low-income housing," I tell him. "Actually, I heard her talking about it at that ladies' night a few months ago, but I didn't know at the time that I would be interested in anything like this."

"Well, maybe Daisy can connect you guys. I'm sure Susan could give you some advice."

"That's a good idea." Rick Moranis has sauntered into the kitchen, looking for food and love, most likely in that order. "What do you think, Ricky?"

"I'm sure he's into it."

After breakfast I stop by Daisy's house to ask her about connecting me with Susan. She's so excited to help that she calls her while I'm still there. Luckily Susan is available for coffee this afternoon. Even though I'm wired from the two cups I've already had with breakfast, I'm eager to talk with her and agree to meet at

The Mud House at one o'clock.

The Mud House is a local coffee shop that I occasionally went to before I started college. It's a funky little shop with local art on the walls and bright blue chairs around reclaimed tables. Even though we're getting together for a meeting, I grab one of the open stools at the front window so I can people-watch. I'm excited to chat with Susan but I'm gonna try to be open-minded and not expect too much to come from this meeting. I'm just glad she's taking the time out to give me some advice.

"Hey, Susan!" I wave my hand to the familiar woman in the yellow dress and sunhat entering the front door.

"Alice! Hi, have you been here long?"

"No, just a few minutes. I wanted to grab these seats. I hope that's okay."

"Of course," she says, placing her tote bag on the stool that reads "Cadet Books" across the front. "Let me go order some tea. I'll be right back." She smiles and leaves me to look out the window where a young family and their toddler are walking by. The boy is riding a tricycle and the man walking slowly behind him is pointing at something across the street, except I can't see what it is.

"So," Susan says when she returns. "Daisy gave me a little background. She says you're looking to start a nonprofit to help girls with math?"

"Yes, well, sort of. So, you know I've been

tutoring, and I got a summer job running creative math camps for girls. It's been going really well, and I even did that workshop with Holly and the other girls."

"Oh, yes. She loved it!" Susan tells me.

"That's great to hear! Well, I wanted to do more things like that. Basically, to get more girls interested in math and, well, get them to like it more."

"That's a tall order," she says sympathetically.

"I know, right?" I ask with a laugh.

"And, who is it you're targeting? Is it low-income families or is it girls who are struggling with math?"

"Both, I suppose. At first, I wanted to reach any girl that needs an opportunity to do something more creative with math. Now I think it would be more beneficial to help girls that have a harder time in a traditional learning environment, especially if they can't afford a tutor."

"Okay," Susan says. She's making notes in a small notebook. "And what's the goal of being a nonprofit? Are you looking for grants?"

"Yes, I want to offer scholarships if parents can't pay for the workshops."

"Well, as you know, I ran a nonprofit to help low-income families get affordable housing. It takes a while to get established. Funding doesn't automatically come in because you're a nonprofit. You have to apply for a lot of grants before you get the support. Plus, nonprofits for women and girls have a harder time getting funding."

"Oh, I see." This is a bit discouraging.

"I can help by showing you where to look and advise you when you start to apply."

"That would be incredible, thank you."

"You might want to get the nonprofit guidelines book," she says. "I forgot what it's actually called. It might be available at the library, or I have an old copy I could lend you. It will give you a checklist of everything you need to know and what you need to do to get started."

"Okay," I say, making notes of what Susan is telling me.

Our conversation lasts about forty-five minutes and I feel overwhelmed by all this information. It's good, of course, but I know this is going to be a huge challenge for me. Plus, I'd like to open the business as soon as I can so I can start making at least a little money. My summer camps are coming to an end next week and I won't have any income for a while.

"Susan, this has been so helpful. Thank you so much for meeting with me and sharing all your advice."

"It's my pleasure. Feel free to reach out again and I'll do the best I can to help."

On the way home, I stop by the library to see if I can find the guidebook that Susan was telling me about. After poking around for a while, I find what I'm looking for. Whoa, this book is seven hundred and ninety-two pages. Good grief! This is going to take me a while.

Flipping through the table of contents, which is alone five pages long, I can already see that there are a few sections I can skip. Good news, I'm down to seven hundred and forty-five pages!

"Alice, hi!" a small but familiar voice comes from behind me.

"Kat! Hi there. How are you?"

"Good," she says. "That's a big book." She points to the massive book open front of me.

"Yeah, it is, isn't it?"

"What is it?"

"Oh, well, it's a book about starting a business."

"Like how I started my soap business?" she asks.

"Well, not exactly. But, sort of. Like yours but bigger."

"That's cool. Can I help? I know a lot about business." That is the sweetest thing ever. I really wish she could help. Maybe I should recruit girls like Kat to work with me. They're our future, after all.

"That's super nice, but it's a little more complicated. I have a lot of new stuff to learn, but you've shown me that hard work always pays off. Certainly, if you can help, I'll be calling!"

This girl is amazing.

18

I'm hosting our first fundraiser today for Girls Count, my new nonprofit. It's been a long and stressful journey, but I'm excited to start spreading the word about my upcoming workshops. I want girls to see how math is used in the real world. I hope that my programs are a way for girls to explore math in a fun and interesting way.

Cullen is inside getting ready and Miranda and Jacob are on their way over. Our fundraiser is a small, intimate gathering at our house. Mostly friends and neighbors are coming, and Daisy has been inviting everyone she knows. Kristen texted me this morning wishing me good luck. Then she made a one-hundred-dollar donation to the website, which was very generous.

"Do you need any help out here?" Cullen asks.

"No, thanks. I'm pretty much set up. Miranda should be here soon anyway."

The raffle table was Daisy's idea. We were so lucky to get several local shops and artisans to donate some items. I'm worried though that we aren't going to get enough people and this whole thing could be for nothing. It's scary putting yourself out there, but we all agreed that if nothing else we'll have a little party in the backyard and celebrate the new business.

"Hey!" calls Miranda as she's walking up the driveway. Jacob has his hands full of bags and Miranda is carrying stacks of Tupperware filled with all sorts of goodies.

"What's all this?" I ask.

"Just some snacks and things that we made. I thought it would be nice for guests to have something to munch on while they mingled."

"I don't know how much mingling there's gonna be. I'm worried no one will show up."

"It's gonna be great! Don't worry," Miranda tries to reassure me.

Dropping their bags and containers on one of the tables, Miranda and Jacob get to work on setting up the food and drinks while my nerves start to take over. I'm having a hard time focusing and I want everything to be perfect.

"Hiya!" calls Daisy.

"Hey," I say. "Daisy, you've met Miranda. This is her fiancé, Jacob."

"Nice to meet you," he says and shakes her hand.

"Daisy is my neighbor," I tell him.

"What can I do to help?" Daisy asks.

"I think we're good," I say. "Feel free to grab

something to eat. Miranda brought food."

I look at my watch. Oh man, ten minutes away and I'm nearly shaking. This is pretty terrifying. I have to actually sell people on this business and try to get them to make a donation for the start-up costs. I've never been much of a salesperson. I want to hide and have someone else do all the talking.

As soon as Cullen comes out of the house Kat and her dad arrive.

"Hey, guys!" I say.

"Hi Alice," says Kat. She's wearing her infamous green Converse shoes today and her hair is growing out and it's a bit messy. This just adds to her cool factor though. She has a very, 'who cares?' attitude that I admire about her. I'm excited for Miranda to finally meet her.

"So, Alice, give us the pitch," Luke says. Oh man, here we go. I tell him all about my plans for Girls Count and why I started a nonprofit. I explain the importance of scholarships and how I want to help families in need. Of course, I've worked with Kat all summer, so he knows how passionate I am about helping girls with math.

"Well, we're very excited about what you're doing, and I'd love to make a donation."

"Wow, thank you so much!" He hands me a check for two hundred and seventy-five dollars, which is the full tuition for one girl to come to summer camp next year. "That's very generous. This will go a long way and it means so much to get your support."

"It's my pleasure. Kat has gotten so much out of working with you. We really hope your business is a success."

My nerves have settled a bit. That felt incredible! I have at least one family on my side and that makes me feel like I'm doing something positive.

Over the next couple of hours, there's a lot of people coming and going and luckily the raffle has done well. It's such a relief that people showed up. I thought the five of us that organized this would all be staring at each other the whole time.

The event is starting to die down and I see Daisy talking with a woman I've never met before. "Alice, this is Jess," she tells me. "She lives a few blocks down and she volunteers at the library with me. You guys should talk. She runs a nonprofit and has been helping start-ups for years."

"Hi Jess, it's nice to meet you," I say.

"You too," she says. "Daisy has told me a lot about you."

"Oh, that's so sweet. She's been my cheerleader since the beginning."

"I'd love to help you in some way if I can. Are you looking to get into schools?"

"Possibly. I tried to run a workshop in one of the public schools, but they weren't too interested in having me there. I guess there's a lot of red tape."

"Yeah, that can be tricky. You have to know

someone inside the school or else it takes forever."

"One school I tried said they wanted programs that are more inclusive and asked if I would consider working with boys too." I was pretty baffled by this response. I mean, I understand where they're coming from, but what would make us stand out? We would just be like any other math program. Didn't boys already have a leg up when it came to mathematics?

"That's kind of weird," she says. "Well, check out the ACT after school program. They work through the Parks Department and I know they're always looking to expand their programming. They offer a lot of free services to low-income families."

"Oh, that sounds perfect!"

Jess hands me her business card and tells me to contact her. What a great resource she could be for me. I've been feeling a little isolated trying to get everything up and running. I read through probably sixty percent of the nonprofit guidebook and it took so many long (unpaid) hours figuring out how to do all this. Having someone to connect with and ask for help is going to save me from a lot of stress.

After chatting with Jess it's time to announce the raffle prize winners. "Hello everyone!" I call out to the remaining guests. "First, I want to thank you all for coming. It means so much to see you here today and share with you my goals for Girls Count. We're going to pick the winners for the prize raffle in just a few minutes."

Kat came back at the end of the fundraiser and was the lucky recipient of a Girls Count gift bag. Inside was a math puzzle book and a sticker set. She was happy to win and even wanted to do some of the puzzles with me.

"This is cool!" she says, pulling out the books and flipping through them. Watching her excitement, she really inspires me and I want her to continue on this journey with me.

"Hey, Kat. What do you think about helping me run a Rube Goldberg Machine workshop? You could be the advisor for some of the girls. Would you want to do that?"

"Um," she says shyly. "Like, I would be a teacher?"

"Yeah, you could work with me and help me run the workshop."

"Sure." She's smiling and acting modest, but I can tell by the look on her face that she's flattered by the idea. She's such a cool kid and I think she would be a great role model for younger girls.

"Cool. I can talk to your parents about it when the time comes and let you know what you need to do."

"Okay," she says. "Thanks Alice."

Inside I plop down on the couch and melt into the cushions. "Oh man, what a day," I say to Cullen.

"Good turnout," he says. "It seems like this was a success."

"Definitely. We had more people show up than I

thought we would. Plus, I received a lot of donations and that's gonna be a huge help moving forward." Rick Moranis takes no time to jump on my lap and settle in. I feel like I could fall asleep right here. With the fundraiser behind me I'm looking forward to the future. Everything has been happening so fast that I haven't had much time to sit and reflect. I can't believe this is really happening. I close my eyes for just a moment, but it doesn't take long before Ricky and I are fast asleep.

19

Today's the big day. My first official Girls Count event is for a group of friends that have been together since preschool. One of the parents reached out to see if I could run a workshop for their group of third and fourth graders. We settled on a three-dimensional project that will help them understand area and volume. Twelve girls are meeting with me this afternoon.

"Are you nervous?" asks Cullen during breakfast.

"Yeah, incredibly nervous. But, I'm excited too. It's gonna be fun. I have a volunteer working with me today. Jess from the fundraiser connected us but I don't know much about her. She used to work for Jess who said she was extremely reliable, sweet, and a hard worker. In fact, those were her words exactly."

"Awesome. It sounds like you're all set."

Gathering all my supplies I'm looking forward to my first official event. I'm nervous about it going well since it's my name on the line, but I'm not nervous about working with the girls. Between the small business workshop and the summer camps, I feel more confident each time I run an event.

When I get to the Helping Hands Community Center, Brenda, the Program Director greets me when I walk in.

"Alice, welcome back," she says.

"Thanks, Brenda. How are you today?"

"Can't complain. You're in the red room today."

"Okay, thank you." Just as I turn the hallway towards my classroom, Brenda calls after me.

"Oh, and someone was looking for you. She's over there," she says, pointing to a young girl who looks a little familiar, but I can't place her.

I walk over to introduce myself. "Hi. I'm Alice. Are you looking for me?" I ask her.

"Yes, I'm your volunteer. Erin Hayes."

"Hayes?" Where have I heard that name before? "Oh my gosh, you're Mrs. Hayes's granddaughter, aren't you? The science teacher?"

"Yes. Did you know her?"

"She was my teacher in elementary school, but it's been quite a few years. How's she doing?"

Erin pauses for a moment, looking down and I can tell something is wrong. "She actually passed away two months ago," she says softly.

"Oh, Erin, I'm so sorry to hear that. Wow. That's terrible news." I'm hit hard by this information and sad to hear that this incredible woman is gone. "I actually wrote her a letter last year when I heard she was sick."

Erin looks back at me. "Wait, you're that Alice?

Mr. Grant at the market gave me your letter. Grandma was so touched by it. She wanted to write back but she was too ill. She couldn't believe one of her students cared that much."

I'm in shock. I wasn't expecting this today and it's getting me choked up. "Really? Oh man, that's so nice. I'm just glad she knew before she passed. She was an incredible teacher and she had a real impact on me. Honestly, part of why I'm here today is because of the way she taught."

Tears are starting to form in Erin's eyes, so I set down the bags that I didn't realize I was still holding and give her a hug. "Erin, I'm so glad you're here today. Let's dedicate today in her memory," I tell her.

"I'd like that."

It's surreal that this is my business. I mean, not only am I in charge but people are here because of something I created. It's an incredible feeling standing here today and after the emotional conversation with Erin, it's a little too much to handle.

Working with girls I've realized how unique each and every one of them is. No two girls are ever alike, and I love seeing how their minds work and how they tackle a problem. This is truly the inspiration for the work I do. Creating a math program that is new and challenging is fun on paper, but once you see the girls working together, there's almost nothing like it. It's so unpredictable and that's why it's so thrilling. I want these young women to have a voice. I want them to feel confident and strong. I want them to know that they count.

Mary Hlastala is the Founder and Executive Director of Girls Count in Portland, OR. To find out more about this organization, visit **www.girlscountpdx.org**.

Made in the USA
Columbia, SC
17 April 2023